THE STORY OF EUCLID

This edition published 2024
by Living Book Press

ISBN: 978-1-76153-170-5 (hardcover)
         978-1-76153-171-2 (softcover)

First published in 1902.

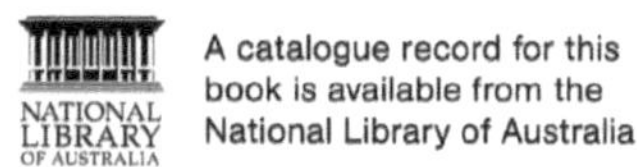

A catalogue record for this book is available from the National Library of Australia

The Story of Euclid

by

WILLIAM BARRETT FRANKLAND

Glossary

To aid the modern reader, this edition of "The Story of Euclid" includes a glossary of terms. Some words may be unfamiliar due to their age or mathematical nature. This glossary aims to clarify their meaning, ensuring a smoother reading experience and a deeper understanding of Euclid's contributions to geometry.

appurtenances: Things that belong to something else as a less important part; additional features or equipment.

mensuration: The process of measuring, especially calculating geometric dimensions like lengths, areas, and volumes.

Megathological: Relating to deep contemplation of grand or lofty ideas, particularly those intended to elevate the mind towards the divine or abstract.

tiro: A beginner or a novice; someone new to learning a particular skill.

parallelopipeds: A solid 3D shape where all six faces are parallelograms (think of a slightly squashed box).

incommensurables: In geometry, this refers to lines or quantities whose lengths don't have a common divisor (or whose ratio cannot be expressed as a fraction of whole numbers). For example, the side of a square and its diagonal are incommensurable.

eleemosynary: Relating to charity or giving freely to those in need.

parallel-axiom: Also called Euclid's Fifth Postulate. It's a fundamental rule in geometry stating: If a line intersects two other straight lines, and the interior angles on the same side add up to less than 180 degrees, then the two straight lines will eventually meet if extended far enough.

Contents

EUCLID

Taken from a Brass Coin in the Repository of the late Queen Christian of Sweden.

Euclid *the Mathematician was of* Alexandria, *where he taught in the Reign of* Ptolemy Lagus *in the* CXX Olympiad *and Year of* Rome 454. *He Wrote many things relating to Musick and Geometry: But his* XV *Books of Elements (of which he is generaly thought to be only the Collector) are most applauded: the two last are attributed to* Hypsicles *of* Alexandria, *and not to him.* Cardan Vossius

PREFACE

THE career of the *Elements* of Euclid has been of an extraordinary and indeed unique character. For two thousand years or more it has served for text-book to countless students, and today it is a work with which all Englishmen are more or less familiar, whilst the name of its writer is a household word throughout the civilized world.

And yet so lacking in curiosity are we of this country, although I do not know that other people have shown themselves much more inquisitive in the matter, that there does not exist, so far as I am aware, any small book of this sort to tell us what in the Story of Euclid is of interest or importance for busy men and women to know. Even in school books, I venture to suggest, there is a quite unaccountable lack of that historical and philosophical information which it is the aim of this little volume in some degree to communicate, and so in writing this brief sketch of Euclidian lore I have had in mind younger as well as older people.

I hope that no one will disapprove of these efforts on the ground that a little knowledge is a dangerous thing; for, whilst I have fears that in points of detail this old-fashioned aphorism may apply only too aptly to myself, it will be a very keen disappointment to me if, in its broad outlines, this panoramic story gives to the reader any essentially wrong impression of the past and present of Euclidian geometry.

Of course the subject labours under the difficulty that occasionally, in order to avoid an unprofitable and insipid vagueness, I have had to resort to downright technical language. Still, should anyone find himself bogged or bored by the abstractness of odd paragraphs, I trust he will see fit to skip the offending places, and return to them after gaining a bird's-eye view of the whole matter.

On the other hand, it may be that some will find it a pleasurable relief, after a hard spell of school work, to stroll in the fields of history, where we almost seem to breathe something of a larger and freer atmosphere, through which great men of past ages appear, moving with a grand and solemn dignity.

I cannot but add a word of thanks to those friends who have assisted me in the correction of proofs and in other ways, especially in the preparation of an index. The works of which I have made use will be found referred to in the course of the book.

W. B. F.
CLARE AND SELWYN COLLEGES,
CAMBRIDGE.
Michaelmas, 1901.

CHAPTER I

INTRODUCTION

Philosophy can bake no bread, but she can procure for us God, freedom, and immortality. - NOVALIS.

ANY one who picks up this little book may ask how the "Story of Euclid" comes to take its place in a "Library of Useful Stories." If his schooltime is past, he may put the question, "Of what use can it be to me to learn any more about a thing for which I never cared but little, and of which I remember not very much?" Or, if his acquaintance with Euclid is still fresh, he may inquire, "How can this story help me, busy as I am with this or that examination?" In fact, at the opening of a new century, time is short, and correspondingly valuable; and this in itself demands that cause be shown why the story of Euclid should be told or read.

It is scarcely credible that very many readers will ever find it possible to turn the contents of such a book as this to account so as to procure for themselves certain pounds, shillings, pence, and farthings sterling. In that sense this story is not at all likely to be useful, though it may still plead usefulness on the ground that it strives to furnish pleasures of a wholesome if quiet sort. Moreover, these pleasures help to invigorate and develop those faculties which brutes do not share; and they may be said to abide rather than to flit, and to enrich rather than to impoverish.

On scientific grounds, further, the story of Euclid has high claims to usefulness. All the great inventions are inseparable from natural science\,: without it there could be none of those mechanical and electrical wonders, at which no one wonders—the steam-engine, the telegraph, the dynamo, and what not. But natural science depends, first and foremost, on measurement; and wherever measurement is made more and more precise, a branch of science is in a fair way to become more and more perfect. And geometry is the science of measurement, in that she is concerned with the how and the why of the rule and compasses, and especially with the art of drawing to scale—only to put forward the simplest service she renders. This story tells how ideas about measurement have changed in the course of time, and so establishes some claim to usefulness from a scientific standpoint.

Then, as already suggested, the story of Euclid introduces questions and problems, at once simple and profound, in which the mind may exercise itself to its full bent. And it seems as if in the complex life which has to be lived today, the mind could not be too strong. Men and women of today, workers in a social scheme, citizens of a vast empire, members of an intelligent humanity, cannot escape the ambition which spurs them on to realize their heritage. No surface knowledge will suffice for those who are "the roof and crown of things." The mind is ever searching for the purpose and inwardness of what it discerns. It may be that this story will prove useful by providing practice in accurate thought about abstract matters.

A very old tale serves well to illustrate the manner in which geometry plunges below the surface. In days before Euclid the plodding student encountered the unpleasant gibe that in proving that two sides of a triangle were together greater than the third, he stated no more than every donkey knew. The fact was well known, so it was derisively observed, to every donkey who walks straight to a bunch of hay. Nevertheless the student had a sufficiently good retort: "Yes, but the donkey does not know the reason why!"

And yet intellectual gymnastics will be far from constituting the chief object of concern; although will be encountered problems, solved and unsolved, which vexed men's minds for many successive generations, still the history of Euclid's great text-book will be the main theme, and the narration of the fates of one of the half-dozen supremely marvellous books the world has seen, through the varied course of twenty-two long centuries. During this prodigious stretch of time the *Elements* have been the very inspired Scripture of mathematics and natural science; and they are still in a position of accepted authority, despite the destructive efforts of criticism. If it is useful to know how the Bible was composed and handed down, as well as to be acquainted with its contents and their significance, it is also useful, in however infinitely less a degree, to learn the story of Euclid.

It might not have been guessed that the history of geometry would march with the history of religion no less than with the history of science, and yet this is the case. Before Christianity had dominated by her own scheme all the highest culture of the world, the subtle restless mind of the pagan Greek strove ceaselessly to read the riddle of life. He looked for the most precise and certain of truths, and found them in geometry, as he thought; he strained his eyes to find in them an ethical teaching to guide him "o'er moor and fen, o'er crag and torrent." There is much pathos in these barren attempts to wring a moral significance out of circles and perpendiculars and numbers.

Far more largely, however, the story of Euclid coincides with the record of the fortunes of science generally, until modern times. Like the rest of science, geometry rose and flourished in Greek soil, and faded awhile in that extra-ordinary and universal blight of thought which the Middle Ages witnessed, when individual opinion was lost and truth came on authority. In things temporal, the feudal system ground man down into a serf; in things spiritual, the ecclesiastical system made that serfdom complete. It is not surprising to see a sign of these black times in the fact that proofs were omitted in the mutilated Euclids which were then current. When what was best in civilization had well-nigh deserted Europe, Euclid, along with all true culture, both of science and of art, found an asylum with an alien race—the Arabs amongst them alone scientific research was unfettered.

Then in due time came the great restoration, a new birth like that proclaimed later with the silver trumpet of a Shelley-

> The world's great age begins anew,
> The golden years return,
> The earth doth, like a snake, renew
> Her winter weeds outworn.

The story of Euclid illustrates clearly the intellectual side of this renewal of life, and casts some light even on its religious side, the so called Reformation, in the conflict of Jesuit and Humanist. With the Renaissance is discerned awakening once more the pure love of knowledge, and that passion for the truth which impels research into the new and criticism of the old. Then, to its shame, the European world had to look to the Arabs for its science; it found its Euclid in Spain, and the first of innumerable printed editions was derived from an Arabic text. "In the year of salvation, 1482," the prolific force of the printing-press made copies of the *Elements* obtainable throughout Western Europe.

Englishmen were neither last nor least in this new striving after exact knowledge and independent thought, and in particular the study of Euclid underwent a vigorous revival, in which others beside professed scholars had a share. Thus the first English printed edition of the *Elements* was the work of a "citizen of London," Henry Billingsley, who modestly apologizes to the learned Universities for trespassing on their preserves; and an eloquent introduction from the pen of John Dee, "an old forworne mathematician," addresses the work, not to "Universitie scholers," but to "the handlyng of unlatined people." This splendid volume, of nearly five hundred folio pages, bears the date 1570; and both earlier and later Englishmen did yeoman service for the better understanding of Euclid.

In the last two centuries most branches of science have undergone revolutionary developments, and geometry is no exception to the rule, though the lines of advance are less widely known. Until lately there would seem to have existed a prevailing impression that geometry, so far as Euclid had formulated it, was stereotyped once for all in the Elements, in a position beyond cavil and criticism. In point of fact, the absolute truth of nearly all Euclid's system is in question; and the concluding chapters of this story will form a commentary on this indisputable if startling statement. There it will be seen that, whereas at the outset geometry is reported to have concerned herself with the measurement of muddy land, she now handles celestial as well as terrestrial problems: she has extended her domain to the furthest bounds of space.

Though the abstractness of geometry may be repugnant to "the natural heart of man," the adoption of the historical method conjures up personalities, and not propositions only. The history of geometry is, as it were, a drama enacted through the centuries therein is beheld the growth of a science from helpless birth and stumbling childhood, through the strenuous but rash vigour of youth, to the perfect wisdom and disciplined strength of manhood. In the life of a science a human life is but an insignificant moment, and from this point of view the history of geometry assumes a grandeur scarcely short of majestic.

CHAPTER II

GEOMETRY FROM BIRTH TO YOUTH

(General Survey, 600-300 B.C.)

The earth beareth fruit of herself; first the blade, then the ear, then the full corn in the ear. - THE GOSPEL.

FROM the third century before the beginning of the Christian era and to a further stage beyond, a single University was mistress of the scientific studies of the world. This queenly University had her seat in the wealthy and populous seaport founded in the Delta of the Nile by Alexander the Great. The city, called Alexandria after its founder, speedily outdistanced all rivals in splendour and opulence, and its University was its proudest boast. The enormous Library, the extensive laboratories and the museums, were thronged by students from all countries, who listened to lectures on philosophy and science.

The chair of geometry was occupied first perhaps by the ablest teacher the University ever had the good fortune to possess: certainly no other teacher has produced a text-book of such lasting merit. The man and the book are, of course, Euclid and his *Elements*, but the book so overshadowed the man that not long after his day Euclid was regularly called the "Elementist." Of his personality little is really known, though some minds may find comfort in the reflections that he is not a myth, that the question of a Proto-Euclid or of a Deutero-Euclid is easily settled, and that no great space needs to be devoted to a Pseudo-Euclid, or any troublesome "other man of the same name."

Euclid may be seen delivering professorial lectures on geometry to Alexandrian students, freshmen and others and very probably these lectures are the basis of a work which he allowed to be copied and circulated under the title *Elements of Geometry.* Others had anticipated him in the composition of such works, and he would be sure to consult some of these earlier treatises; perhaps they would be contained in the nucleus of the Library. Thus the inquiry is started: How much did Euclid borrow or rearrange, and how much did he himself contribute? And it will be of interest to learn who were the pioneers whose work was used, and how they too acquired their knowledge. The settlement of these points means an investigation of the rise and progress of geometry before Euclid's day, which will be undertaken in succeeding chapters, whilst the present is devoted to a general sketch.

All traditions unite in declaring that the birth of geometry took place in Egypt. Its prime cause was understood to consist in the practical necessity of surveying lands flooded by the Nile, and this is told in his quaint way by John Dee, writing some years before the time of the Armada. He says:

"This science of magnitude, his properties, conditions, and appurtenances, commonly now is, and from the beginning hath of all philosophers been, called Geometry. But, verily, with a name too base and scant for a science of such dignity and ampleness. And perchance that name, by common and secret consent of all wise men, hitherto hath been suffered to remain, that it might carry with it a perpetual memory of the first and notablest benefit by that science to common people showed:

"Which was, when bounds and meres of land and ground were lost and confounded, as in Egypt yearly with the over-flowing of Nilus, the greatest and longest river in the world, upon these and such like occasions, some by ignorance, some by negligence, some by fraud, and some by violence, did wrongfully limit, measure, encroach, or challenge, by pretence of just content and measure, those lands and grounds; and so great loss, disquietness, murder, and war did full often sue, till by God's mercy and man's industry the perfect science of lines, planes, and solids, like a divine justiciar, gave unto every man his own.

"The people then by this art pleasured, and greatly relieved in their land's just measuring; and other philosophers writing rules for land-measuring; between them both thus confirmed the name of Geometry, that is, according to the very etymology of the word, Land-measuring."

To the Egyptians is thus assigned the credit of the beginnings of geometry some unknown number of centuries before Christ; and at the least it is certain that the Greeks took the cue from them. Through imposing a narrow meaning on the word "useful," the Egyptian mind advanced no further than a few rules of thumb. From their short book of mensuration the Greeks extracted a page, and copied it but the copy was infinitely more valuable than the original. The agile and energetic Greek temperament, devoted to science for its own sake, needed no more than a beckoning hand towards realms for conquest.

To be just, the Egyptians were able to effect a good deal beside this reported recovery of boundaries obliterated by mud: they had geometrical rules applicable to religious ends. Immemorial temples are found to have had their sites pitched with an exceptional care, so that their situation with reference to the heavenly bodies might be true; and so, in the ecclesiastical, as well as in the civil world, the Egyptians had a fund of "useful" geometry. But in this confinement of scope to the "useful" all hope of progress died; and, for all they cared, knowledge might have continued in the same state for another thousand years.

True Geometry was begotten when the Greek thinker, Thales, left his home on the shores of Asia Minor, and travelled far and wide, partly for the sake of commerce, but more from a restlessness which was the sign of awakening life. It is twenty-five centuries since Thales visited Egypt, and then, as now, that mysterious country exercised all the fascinations of an inscrutable antiquity. Above all, its priests, charged with the cherished and hidden traditions of ages, must have excited the admiration of the philosopher to him they would represent the highest culture of an ancient nation; and from them he learned their rough-and-ready geometrical methods which, on his return, he investigated in a more abstract manner. The discoveries thus made will be detailed later: here may be simply recorded the titles bestowed on him by his compatriots: The Ancient, The Sage, The Father of Philosophy. Thales is not only the father of geometry, but of all science.

Since it is proposed at present only to sketch briefly the progress of geometry before Euclid, only the most brilliant of the Elementist's forerunners will be mentioned. Among these, Pythagoras belonged to the generation following Thales.

Gathering about himself a band of disciples, he founded a veritable college, endowed with much genius and little money. His personality is more shadowy than might otherwise have been the case, because of a peculiar custom of his followers. For long after his death they formed an exclusive sect, with "plain living and high thinking" for their rule of life. Pushing humility and loyalty to the extreme, they ascribed all their discoveries to "the Master," as they |were wont to call him. The formula, the Master said, has become a proverb, and it is impossible not to admire such devotion, though it hides the real Pythagoras from modern eyes.

The best known among the names of the other great pioneers is that of Plato, but it must not be forgotten that his fame was not earned in geometrical fields. The "Divine Philosopher" received a mathematical education of the highest excellence, such as might be balanced today by courses at English, German, and French Universities. His keenness for geometry was great, and his enthusiasm lasting; indeed, his admiration for geometrical studies is shown by the warning placed by him over the door of his Academy[1]

No entrance to the ungeometrical.

In his ideal Republic, geometry is to receive the attention it deserves, because it is "the knowledge of that which is everlasting." Hereon John Dee soliloquizes in words which are peculiarly impressive in their eloquence:

---

1   The building in which he lectured at Athens, about 400 B.C., and which has given its name to similar institutions.

This was Divine Plato his judgment, both of the purposed, chief, and perfect use of geometry, and of his second depending derivative commodities. And for us Christian men a thousand, thousand more occasions are to have need of the help of megathological contemplations, whereby to train our imaginations and minds, by little and little, to forsake and abandon the gross and corruptible objects of our outward senses, and to apprehend by sure doctrine demonstrative, things mathematical.

The fourth century before the era of Grace was rich in talented geometers, all of Greek blood, who pushed geometrical knowledge into regions far beyond the range of the *Elements*. In fact, Euclid's book was devised for beginners, and contained but a tithe of the geometry known to the great teacher: it would comprise only as much as he judged appropriate to the end he had in view, that is, to furnish an introduction to geometry, and to attain a certain goal in his last book.

Such is in brief the course of geometrical discovery up to Euclid's day. In the three succeeding chapters will be examined more leisurely what has been rapidly reviewed, but two facts call for more immediate remark.

First, the science of geometry did not spring into existence full-grown from the brain of Euclid, as the goddess Minerva was fabled to have emerged in perfect womanly form from the head of Jupiter. The *Elements* were in germinal life centuries before Euclid's birth, when the seed was transplanted by Thales from Egypt. It was then an apparently weakly and insignificant thing, but planted in Greek soil it sprouted, and in the time of the Pythagorean Brotherhood came to have a beautiful if diminutive form. After their day it passed by successive gradations into the full-grown tree, the sturdy and shapely oak which Euclid revealed to the world. Geometrical history is incomprehensible apart from evolutionary principles.

Secondly, the legion of lost works on geometry, both prior and subsequent to Euclid's day, are witnesses to the survival of the fittest. Euclid took from earlier works what he thought good to repeat and perpetuate. Then these earlier works died that the *Elements* might live, and gained no more than that shadowy kind of immortality described by a German novelist,[2] an immortality resting on the fact that a person's ideas live on more or less in the minds of generations to come. On the other hand, later works did not achieve even this much: unable successfully to combat the *Elements*, they went down under Euclid's victorious chariot-wheels.

Although it was principally in revision and arrangement that Euclid's work consisted, the chiefest mathematicians since the composition of the *Elements* have seen in them the working of a supremely masterly mind.

---

2   Gustav Freytag, in his "Lost Manuscript: " but the view has not been without lofty and generous exposition in the world of English literature.

CHAPTER III

THE FATHER OF GEOMETRY
(660-550 B.C.)

He was happy, if to know
Causes of things be happiness.
M. ARNOLD.

IT is now time to proceed to a closer view of the pioneers who lived and worked for the furtherance of geometrical truth in the three centuries before Euclid, and the present chapter will be devoted to the first of them—Thales, the founder of geometry.

Born at the dawn of European civilization, when its earliest rays were coming from the East, Thales was a native of Miletus, a flourishing Greek city on the Western shores of Asia Minor, between which and Greece proper lay—

The Isles of Greece,
Where burning Sappho loved and sung,
Where grew the arts of war and peace.

He soon became famous for a knowledge and wisdom which gave him rank among the Seven Sages, and of his acumen and enterprise many fireside tales were told.

One of these stories speaks of a mule possessed of the undesirable habit of lying down in the stream when a ford was crossed. As the burden was composed of salt, the animal's behaviour did some credit to its reasoning powers, and may not have been entirely due to perversity. But Thales was astute enough to effect a complete cure by loading the mule for several journeys with nothing but sponges. He is also reported once to have made a corner in olives by buying up a whole year's produce, which he then sold at his own price, thus inaugurating, if the tale is not idle, one of the nefarious practices of modern commerce.

During the earlier part of a long life, Thales visited Egypt, where his passion for knowledge exercised itself in such wise that he quickly exhausted the slender stock of mensuration in the possession of the Egyptian priests. Six hundred years before Christ is a not improbable date to assign to the visit, and it may be recollected that a little previously Egypt was still a closed empire, like the China of a few years ago. The sphinx-like character of the nation, its antiquity and mystery, impressed the Greek visitor and priests of a cult which extended back for uncounted generations could patronize their guests and declare, "You are but children." Children were Thales and his contemporaries, indeed, but they grew fast, and soon outstripped a civilization that had reached its dotage.

Lower Egypt was, and is, practically rainless. Only the irrigation of the Nile in its annual flood kept back the encroaching desert-sand: but for its regular overflow desolation was doomed to reign supreme over a land smiling with crops and bedecked with dwellings.

Year by year Father Nile overflowed his banks, and fertilized with rich mud fields far and wide. To know the time of this visitation, and to retrace the lost boundaries, [3] were problems for the ruling class, and which some time or other had been faced successfully by the priests. It would be easy to exaggerate the extent of the priestly code of learning, since the thicker the mist, the greater do things loom; the high-water-mark of their geometry was doubtless attained in their knowledge that—

If the sides of a triangle measure 3, 4 and 5, then the greatest angle is a right angle.

This fact was of use to them in the erection of temples facing the proper point of the heavens. Above, they saw moving serenely and resolutely across the sky the bright emblems of a Power demanding their adoration; and towards these their sacred buildings looked at fitting seasons of the year. In plotting out such sites, cords of lengths as specified above were pegged out on level ground, and the right angle so constructed afforded them much assistance. Why the angle should be right, the Egyptian mind very probably neither knew nor cared.

This, and much like it, Thales the Wise would learn with avidity, though the materialism and guesswork of the Egyptians might leave him extremely dissatisfied. In his mind the Egyptian cords were refined until they became Greek lines: the place of the concrete cord was taken by the abstract idea of length without breadth or thickness, and thus may have been born the notion of a "line," now so familiar and then so strange.

---

3   De Morgan chose to scoff at this tradition of the beginning of geometry. Calling it the "stock" history, he quoted the couplet-

> To teach weak mortals property to scan
> Down came Geometry, and formed a plan!

Things went pretty much the same way in the science of astronomy. The Egyptians observed eclipses as they came round annually, made notes of the occasions, and registered them. Another Oriental nation, the Chaldeans, kept like records, though with greater fruit in their discovery of the extraordinary fact that eclipses repeat themselves after an interval of eighteen years plus eleven days.[4] But it was left to Thales and Western minds to pierce below appearances: Thales sowed the seed of which Galileo and Newton gathered the increase.

The mensuration which he learned from the Egyptians, Thales purified, making out of their practice his theory. To them he would seem a dreamer, an academician remote from the realities of a busy pushing world. Their desire did not extend beyond that knowledge of which they clearly perceived the proximate utility; he appears rather to have loved knowledge for its own sake, apart from the good things to be immediately and obviously gained from it. And yet (gain coming, as ever, by loss) Thales has proved a greater benefactor of the entire human family than all the Egyptian priests with all their practical rules.

From Egypt, Thales returned to his native city, and there enjoyed the calm of the study after the bustle of the market. Yet so comprehensive was his genius that to the end of his life his interest in public affairs was maintained. Meanwhile a little band of eager students attached themselves to "the Father of Geometry," and after his death, not far from 550 B.C., his teaching lived on in the school he had thus founded.

In one sense, the contributions to geometry made by Thales

4   In this way future eclipses were predicted from a knowledge of those past.

are of inestimable value. He was its very founder, and thereby the founder of most of the exact sciences: it is therefore difficult to exaggerate his rank in the Story of Euclid. Not only did he make a successful start, but progress of considerable sort is attributed to him. Naturally, most of his discoveries are transparent to the modern eye; it seems, for instance, so very obvious that—

A circle is bisected by its diameter;

and yet, in early hours, when morning vapours obscured the student's sight, this simple theorem must have been a day-star. It meant so much: for the very idea of a "circle" was new—a "line," and not a piece of cord. "Diameter" corresponded to a special sort of line, which was called "straight;" and this straight line might be drawn anyhow provided only that it passed through a particular "point," the "centre" of the circle. From the coarse practicality of the Egyptians to this pitch of abstract thought is an immense step, only possible to a mind of Thales' titanic power.

Thales is also reported to have taught that—

If a triangle have two sides of equal lengths, then two of its angles are equal.[5]

Now Euclid's proof of this statement is notoriously hard, and this invites the question what proof Thales gave, and whether Euclid's "Pons Asinorum" is an elaboration of a cruder piece of work by Thales. Although it is not entirely certain, yet

---

5   As Euclid expresses it in his fifth proposition: "The angles at the base of an isosceles triangle are equal."

very probably no injustice is done to Thales if he is represented as giving no rigorous proof of his statements. This failing is in the nature of a defect, and it has to be confessed, therefore, that Thales was less than superhuman. His geometrical truths were discovered in his own way, and may have been taught to others as rules or dogmas. On this account the beginnings of geometrical knowledge rather than of geometrical science ought to be ascribed to Thales; and the latter must then be linked to the name of Pythagoras.

From Thales, moreover, comes the theorem given fifteenth among the propositions of Euclid's first book—

If two straight lines intersect, the vertically opposite angles are equal.[6]

But the grandest discovery attributed to him is undoubtedly this—

The angle in a semicircle is a right angle.[7]

Though neither of these statements would appear to have been proved by its discoverer, yet the knowledge of the latter theorem is an extremely striking achievement. It is hard to suppose that Thales merely surmised its truth: it has been considered to be a conscious inference from that greatest theorem in geometry—

The three angles of a triangle are together equal to two right angles.[8]

6   Euc. i. 15.
7   Euc. iii. 31.
8   Euc. i. 32.

At the very least Thales must have had an inkling of this; although he may not have been possessed of that sceptical spirit which is the handmaid of true Science, and serves her by withholding or deferring credence to what is not proven. In a word, in the dawn of geometry, instinct cannot be divorced from reason.

Thales was very far from being a mere theorist: the abstract truths he obtained, he applied to questions of practical interest. For instance, history relates how he "measured the pyramids, making an observation of his shadow when it was of the same length as himself, and applying it to the pyramids." Even to those in charge of it, the height of a pyramid must have been a puzzling matter.[9] The riddle was solved by Thales, who waited some afternoon till his shadow was as long as himself and then measured the length of the shadow of the pyramid on the level plane about it. This length he concluded to be the height of the edifice; and plausibly enough, for does it not "stand to commonsense"? Probably this would have been all the proof Thales could give, though Euclid would have spoken of "similar triangles."

Another hopeless puzzle to the Egyptian mind would be the estimation of the distance of a ship at sea. Thales, it is stated, devised some way of effecting this: probably he observed the bearings of the ship from two different spots ashore, and then drew a diagram to scale.

This, then, is about all—perhaps, as Froude would say, more than all—that can be said to be known about Thales, the first

9   As regards the interest taken by the Greeks in so strange and foreign an object as a pyramid, see p. 47. Thales was acquainted with Euc. i. 26.

geometer. Whatever doubts remain, this much is established beyond controversy, that Thales was the Columbus of a New World, that vast and rich domain of the exact sciences, the exploration of which has so mightily increased the sum-total of human knowledge and human worthiness.

CHAPTER IV

THE MASTER AND THE BROTHERHOOD

(550-450 B.C.)

Here, through the feeble twilight of this world
Groping.

TENNYSON.

IN an exquisite passage Vergil narrates the promise of the gods, that if the golden bough be torn from the mystical tree, another is not lacking. Yet when Thales died there was none ready to fill his place: successors indeed were found, but their services were of no great help to geometry. Much of the thought of the time was devoted to ineffable speculations about the cosmos.

For Pythagoras was reserved the honour of raising Thales' geometry to the full dignity of a science. Early in life he had known the great Ionian teacher, but had not attached himself to his school. His career (575-500 B.C.) embraced most of the sixth century before Christ; and on a cloud of uncertainty his personality is projected to heroic breadth and height. Yet it is a matter of certainty that few men have impressed upon others to an equal degree their purposes and aims. For many scores of years his disciples held together in a compact and loyal brotherhood, and attributed to him their discoveries, small and great. Their knowledge and their traditions were maintained inviolate, and fully revealed to the neophyte only after a three years' probation, of silent study on his part, and of approving scrutiny on theirs.

Tradition has much to say about the life of Pythagoras, and it would be harsh to dismiss it as unhistorical. He was born of Phoenician parents at Samos, one of the isles of Greece not far distant from the birthplace of Thales. He travelled in Egypt and Chaldxa, the reputed homes of hidden lore; and, while still young, lectured at Samos. But he lectured with scanty success, for the times were changing. It was the age of the tyrannical Crossus, and in less prosperous days the Ionian youths had less leisure. So, "following the current of civilization,"[10] Pythagoras migrated to the rich cities of Southern Italy, where, first at Tarentum and then at Croton, he fell in with congenial citizens of Greater Greece. The gilded youth attached themselves enthusiastically to their teacher; indeed, so close was the bond between them, that his mathematical or philosophical school bade fair to merge into a secret society. Nor was the glamour of romance wanting to complete the picture, for among his hearers was a beautiful and cultured lady, in whom he found a devoted wife.

All this the democratic party beheld with fierce indignation, and came to consider Pythagoras a dangerous foe. His school was thronged by aristocratic audiences, and these they suspected of assembling for purposes of political intrigue. The jealousy of the mob compelled him finally to leave Crotona

---

10   The reader is referred to Mr. Allman's *Greek Geometry from Thales to Euclid*, which has been generally followed in the third, fourth, and fifth chapters.

for Metapontum. According to one tradition, the mad fool-fury of demagogues finally pursued him to death; but more pleasant is the tradition which records that he ended his life tranquilly among his beloved studies.[11]

Such is the gist of the eventful history of Pythagoras' career: it displays a man compassing the earth in search of knowledge, and sacrificing all to ensure its perpetuation. A pretty story reveals his personality with some clearness, and illustrates this trait in his character. He is at Samos, eager to gain pupils but pupils do not come, and, for a makeshift, he is obliged to pay an artisan wages in order to secure at least this audience. Afterwards, pretending to fall into poorer circumstances, the enthusiastic geometer is gratified to have his pupil offer to pay an equal remuneration to have the lessons in geometry continued. With this story the motto of the Brotherhood may have some connection—

> A figure and a step onward:
> Not a figure and a florin.

At all events, the motto is a lasting witness to a very singular devotion to knowledge for its own sake.

The views entertained by Pythagoras on the spiritual and bodily economy of man in connection with metempsychosis or vegetarianism hardly call for discussion; it is more interesting to note his conviction that the earth rotated,[12] though he does not appear to have been aware that the planet moves about the

---

11   A sketch of Pythagoras' life was written by Theano, but unhappily has been lost.
12   It must be remembered, however, that there is a risk of assigning credit to Pythagoras for what his followers actually achieved, because their rule was to refer all their teaching to him, the Master. See below, p. 28.

sun. The latter "step onward" was not taken for two thousand years, when Copernicus proclaimed it, and Galileo proved it.

Pythagoras was by no means a mere geometer at heart he was both philosopher and moralist. Without and within himself he searched below the surface, and his view of the world directed his geometrical research. The Ionian teachers had reduced the world in thought, till it rested upon a few broad principles. With the assumption of four elements, they were prepared to build up the fabric of Nature, for the world, according to their view, was composed only of Fire, Earth, Air, and Water in various mixtures. This speculation, plausible as it is, does not find acceptance at the present time, when the number of elements is generally reckoned to be far greater than four; but the old idea that these elements were built up of atoms has survived, and still proves useful in some departments of science.

According to the Greek thinkers, these four kinds of atoms, fiery, earthen, aerial, and watery, were of distinct shapes, but all in their way perfectly regular and symmetrical. Sooner or later, it was found that there were five such shapes that a symmetrical solid might take, namely, the Tetrahedron, the Cube, the Octahedron, the Icosahedron, and the Dodecahedron. Then the idea arose that atoms of Fire were of tetrahedral shape; atoms of Earth, of cubical shape; atoms of Air, of octahedral shape; and atoms of Water, of icosahedral shape. In this way all the shapes of the "regular solids" were disposed of among the various elements, except the dodecahedron; and this, for that it was the most mysterious of all, represented to them the world as a whole. In the language of the mystic, it recapitulated the universe into itself. One might well say of this view, in Tennyson's words—

All the phantom Nature stands,
A hollow form with empty hands.

In this vein ran the speculations, which led Pythagoras, or his followers, to the study of the regular solids; from such a point of view it was distinctly worthwhile to prosecute such research, and doubtless the lifework of many a nameless Pythagorean Brother went towards the successful termination of the quest. In those early days the innermost secrets of nature lay in the lap of geometry, and the extraordinary inference follows that Euclid's *Elements*, which are devoted to the investigation of the regular solids, are therefore in reality and at bottom an attempt to "solve the universe." Euclid, in fact, made this goal of the Pythagoreans the aim of his *Elements*.

In forming an estimate of Pythagoras' work it has to be noted how many projects may have been left unfinished by him, and have been carried out later by the members of the Brotherhood. Thus there arises a danger of assigning too much to the Master to whom his followers assigned all. Still it cannot be far wrong to suppose that it was Pythagoras' wont to insist upon proofs, and so to secure that rigour which gives to mathematics its honourable position among the sciences. First of all, there were some theorems discovered by Thales which stood in need of proof. It was proved for the first time by the Master, or one of the Brotherhood, that-

The sum of the angles of a triangle is two right angles.

It is a great pity that the original proof is lost, for it would have been highly interesting to see how they bridged the abyss where Euclid uses the parallel-axiom.[13]

On a discovery of Thales' already mentioned an old commentator writes: "For this theorem and many others, thanks be to Thales the Ancient. For he is said to have been the first to realise and declare that in every isosceles triangle the angles at the base are equal; though what is now called 'equal' was of old called 'similar.'" It seems very probable that Pythagoras succeeded in devising a proof of this as of other of Thales' geometrical truths.

If the reader will refer to the forty-fourth proposition of Euclid's first book he will encounter a problem said to have been solved first by Pythagoras. The event was esteemed so great a triumph that the Master celebrated it by the sacrifice of an ox.

But Pythagoras' supreme achievement is recorded a little later in the *Elements*. In his first book Euclid works up to a climax, which he reserves for the end. The last proposition but one is the forty-seventh, and of the earlier theorems surprisingly few are not necessary for its proof.[14] This Theorem of the Squares is a geometrical truth of unique beauty and extreme significance, and its discovery has always been ascribed to Pythagoras; how he was led to it remains matter of conjecture, for Euclid's neat proof must be an afterthought.

The Pythagorean theorem (Euc i, 47) marks the first stage of the journey towards the construction of the regular solids.

13   See below, p. 56.
14   This should by no means be taken on trust. It is not hard to draw up a list of propositions in the first book of Euclid, which are not necessary, somehow or other, for the proof of Euc. i. 47.

One of these, the dodecahedron,[15] had an irresistible fascination for the Pythagorean; and correspondingly attractive to him was the flat five-sided "regular pentagon." For example, the mystical emblem of health, which the Brethren employed, was derived from this figure, by producing the sides to form a five-rayed star. A story is told of this badge, that a journeying Pythagorean fell ill at some remote way-side inn, and was nursed by the landlord, though in vain. Having no money with which to repay his host's kindness, he scrawled the five-rayed star on a board, and bade him hang it up outside the inn. Soon after the death of the sick man, a stranger rode up, and, on seeing the board, dismounted instantly and made inquiries, as the result of which the landlord found himself amply rewarded for his charity to a Brother in distress.

Even after making a considerable allowance for his pupils' share, the Master's geometrical work calls for much admiration. His achievements in arithmetic, music, and astronomy cannot be estimated here; suffice it to say that everywhere he appears to have inaugurated genuinely scientific methods, and to have laid the foundations of a high and liberal education. For nearly a score of centuries, to the very close of the Middle Ages, the four Pythagorean subjects of study—arithmetic, geometry, astronomy, music—were the staple educational course, and were bound together into a fourfold way of knowledge—the Quadrivium.

During the century of their existence the Brotherhood worked out the substance of Euclid's first and second books,

15   This was a solid enclosed by twelve flat faces, each of which had five equal sides and five equal angles, that is, was a regular pentagon.

as well as a good deal of the fourth and sixth. A strange gap manifests itself, however; the theory of the circle, of which Euclid's third book is full, was not the object of the attention to be expected from the fact that Pythagoras called the circle the most beautiful of plane figures. And, further, the methods of the fifth book, which have been esteemed especially subtle, did not come to Euclid from the Pythagoreans, but from Eudoxus the Illustrious, whose name and fame Euclid's have unduly obscured.

Throughout peace and persecution the Brotherhood held close for a century or more, and to the last it was impious for any member of the community to take to himself the credit of fresh discoveries. Thus Hippasus was thought to have perished at sea simply because he boasted that he had constructed the Dodecahedron: he ought to have ascribed all the honour to the Master. But in the fourth century before Christ times had changed, and publicity became desirable. So it came to pass that Philolaus wrote his "Tradition about Pythagoras" for the Athenian public in the first half of that century; his work comprised the essentials of the Pythagorean system of knowledge, and is all but entirely lost.

CHAPTER V

THE ILLUSTRIOUS GEOMETER

(450-300 B.C.)

With aching hands and bleeding feet
We dig and heap, lay stone on stone;
We bear the burden and the heat
Of the long day, and wish 'twere done.
Not till the hours of light return
All we have built do we discern.
                    MATTHEW ARNOLD.

THE time of trial for Greece came to an end about 480 B.C., when the Persian yoke was thrown off and trampled underfoot. Athens had led in war, and in peace she still retained her headship over a free Hellas. A period of prosperity and progress ensued, scarcely interrupted by the internecine Thirty Years' War in which Sparta and Athens became engaged.

Hippocrates was born in Chios, another of those Isles of Greece which have been frequently mentioned, during the last throes of the Persian War. For some time he was occupied in mercantile pursuits, but his commercial career came to a sudden and ignominious close. Whether it was at the hands of pirates or of unscrupulous customs-collectors, he lost most of his wealth, and resorted to Athens in the hopes of obtaining reparation for the wholesale robberies he had suffered. Disappointed and ridiculed, he was fain to solace himself with the study of geometry, and enlisted as a Pythagorean. Because of his poverty, the Order allowed him to keep the wolf from the door by teaching for fees. This was contrary to the Master's maxim—

> A figure and a step onward:
> Not a figure and a florin,—

but the Brotherhood seem to have deemed it a greater crime to acquire fame than money.

Hippocrates disbursed more than he received in things geometrical. Though of a dull and heavy appearance, he possessed extraordinary powers of mind, and it will be seen in a later chapter how important were his contributions to the solution of two of those three great historic problems,[16] which exercised the minds of successive geometers for some centuries.

A beautiful discovery about the sizes of certain crescent-shaped figures, called "lunules," is due to Hippocrates, but his greatest services consist in the improvement of method. His "step onward" in this direction is simple and important in the highest degree, for he is said to have been the first to display clearly the manner in which geometrical truths depend on one another. Under his hands geometry became, from being a miscellaneous collection of sporadic facts, a compact system of organized truth. His plan was to start from the simplest things, and deduce from them more and more complex results until the most abstruse theorems were deduced. This is precisely the procedure with which Euclid has familiarised the world by adopting it in his *Elements*; it is hard indeed

---

16   See below, Chapter X. Whilst of no great importance in themselves, these problems led to the development of the higher parts of Geometry.

to imagine geometry a mere random collection of scattered instances; and, indeed, ever since Hippocrates' day, the science has been an organic whole, "compacted of that which every joint supplieth." It is a thousand pities that his work, written on these lines, and in a sense the first elementary text-book on geometry, should have been ground out of existence by the adamantine *Elements* of Euclid.

Hippocrates' life embraces the second half of the fifth century before Christ. Of Archytas, who next comes under mention, the date is not fully known, though he flourished a century before Euclid, about 400 B.C.

Archytas was born at Tarentum, one of the opulent Greek colonies in South Italy visited by Pythagoras; and rose to be one of the most influential citizens of that powerful city. His soldierly and statesmanlike qualities secured him repeated re-election to the office of commander-in-chief, despite the law which forbade the same man to retain the office for more than a single year. The trust was not misplaced, for he was never defeated in battle. In his private life it is permitted to catch glimpses of a gentle and lovable man, fond of children and considerate to his slaves; and he may be seen devising a toy for the amusement of infants. His amiable character displays itself on a grander scale outside the domestic world. In 360 B.C. he was instrumental in saving the life of his friend Plato, who had irritated Dionysius the Elder beyond the endurance of that tyrant: the friendship of Archytas and Plato was, indeed, a proverb. By the hand of God the death of this great and good man was as tragical as his life was happy. He perished by shipwreck in the Adriatic Sea.

Thee, that wouldst measure the sea and the land
And reckon the number of numberless sand,
    (A handful of earth on thy head!)
Thee, that exploredst celestial things,
And soaredst so high on thy fanciful wings,
    It profiteth naught. (Thou'rt dead!)

Himself a pupil of Philolaus, Archytas furthered and promulgated the geometrical knowledge of the Pythagoreans. But their day was done; and as their secrets became open their numbers dwindled, though the publication of their hoarded knowledge was not made without angry sputterings from the more conservative of the Brethren. Some actually went so far as to see in his violent end a visitation upon Archytas from offended deities for his impiety. His geometrical discoveries will be related incidentally; it may be mentioned here that he was the instructor of the illustrious Eudoxus, and he was also the first to make geometrical use of lines which are not flat but winding, like a screw.

Democritus was a philosopher and mathematician of parts, whose life extended from about 460 to 370 years B.C. It is possible that antiquity took him at his own valuation; his reputation was truly great, but a description he gave of his geometrical powers was nothing short of impressive. Plato was desirous of an opportunity to burn all the writings of this "laughing philosopher," as he was called, and, if times have not changed, this may help to account for his fame. Possibly his work has been largely incorporated in that of later writers like Euclid; at present its value can be perceived only by an exercise of the imagination.

Even the case of Plato (429-348 B.C.) is not very different, for his "Divine Philosophy" gained him a fame which led to exaggeration of his geometrical exploits. There has continually prevailed a notion that Plato played a leading part in the development of geometry, but the idea has been exploded, one might say. "An assumption," "a legend," are the judgments of two critics[17] who have threshed out the whole matter, and it is asserted that in mathematics Plato was "painstaking rather than inventive." It may be observed that Eudemus, the historian of geometry, is guarded in his allusion to him; Plato, he says, "contributed to the progress of geometry and of the other mathematical sciences, through his evident zeal for these subjects, and the mathematical matter introduced into his writings."

It is not pleasant to detract from a great man's name, but Plato's reputation can well afford to be shorn of an exaggerated geometrical fame, and Aristotle's words are appropriate :-

Plato is a friend of mine, but Truth a greater still.

If indeed Plato is to be lauded as of yore, what epithets can be found strong enough for the deserts of an Eudoxus or a Menxechmus? Nevertheless one of the most eminent men the world has produced cannot be passed over without some sketch of his life.

Plato was an Athenian by birth, but he received a cosmopolitan education. When he was some thirty years old his teacher, Socrates, was condemned to drink the poisonous cup, and this sad event drove him from Greece, east, south, and west, in search of knowledge. A diligent student of math-

17   Mr. Allman and M. Tannery, writing in 1884 and 1887 respectively.

ematics, endowed with unique opportunities, he must have acquired an unique knowledge. As has been seen, he was an intimate friend of Archytas; and he was also the familiar friend of the great Eudoxus. The former he visited at Tarentum the latter was his companion in Egypt. About a score of years were spent in thus ascertaining all that was being taught up and down the world, and Plato then returned to his native city, there to found a college, the everlastingly famous "Academy."

Plato is said to have had Pythagorean sympathies, and one symptom thereof evinced itself in the well-known warning inscribed over the door of the Academy,—

No entrance to the ungeometrical.

He insisted on the ideal side of geometry, and would not tolerate mechanical constructions. Archytas and Eudoxus were severely reproved by him for giving solutions of the Delian Problem [18] by means of apparatus more complicated than ruler and compasses. History does not record whether these experts rebelled against his tyranny: at any rate, succeeding generations took Plato very seriously in this matter.

For a time Plato studied under a certain philosopher, Euclid of Megara, who, by a curious mistake, was confused by editors of the Middle Ages and beyond, with Euclid the Elementist. The error prevailed for a while after the invention of printing, and some of the beautiful early folios of Euclid's works have their title-pages marred by this mistake. Apparently Commandinus, in the year 1572, was the first editor to set the matter right; and thus Euclid of Megara was stripped

18   See below, Chapter X.

of the Alexandrian plumes with which he had been wrongly decorated for a season.

Next appears a singularly versatile and accomplished man, the Illustrious Eudoxus, whose life covers the range 408-355 B.C. Born in Crete, he studied for some years under Archytas, like Plato; and with Plato he travelled in Egypt. The distinguished pair of young men made a stay at Heliopolis, taking up their residence with the priests, and during that period a portentous event came to pass. Eudoxus was present at some temple service, when the sacred bull was observed to lick his garment. This ominous event foreboded both good and ill, according to the priests Eudoxus, they prophesied, would be "endoxos," that is, illustrious; but he would also be short-lived. The discernment of the priests was very remarkable; Eudoxus did become illustrious, and died all too soon. But, alas, his reputation was short-lived also; and, rightly or wrongly, the glory of Euclid hid him from the view of posterity,—unless the simpler explanation is accepted, that his greatness failed to strike the popular fancy.

On his return to Europe Eudoxus settled in a charming and secluded spot on the shores of the Sea of Marmora, and there built an astronomical observatory. It is surprising to discover further that his mathematical knowledge was rivalled by his acquaintance with medicine and jurisprudence. When he visited Athens its townsmen received him with enthusiasm, and Plato renewed his friendship with him. The learned visitor was accompanied by many of his pupils, of whom one at least, Menrechmus, belonged to the first rank of geometers. Eudoxus and his company resided at the Academy; and this brilliant sojourn perhaps gave to that institution a reputation for mathematical studies, which otherwise it could not have managed to gain. It was there that he met Aristotle "the Superhuman;' the two men differed in their views on some fundamental matters, and it is therefore pleasing to find the latter testifying spontaneously to the purity and loftiness of Eudoxus' character. When Eudoxus died, he was in the flower of his age.

No one can fail to remark the powerful influence exerted by Egypt upon the minds of the pioneers of Euclid. Thales, in the first place, estimated the heights of pyramids; and now Eudoxus estimated their volumes. He showed, in fact, that the volume of a pyramid is precisely the area of the base multiplied by a third of the height, and he saw that the same held good whatever the shape of the base were. These results of his were summed up by Euclid in several propositions of the twelfth book of the *Elements*.

In earlier days the Pythagoreans[19] and others had tried to build up a sound theory of proportion, a theory that should be applicable all round, not only to ordinary numbers, but also to numbers that cannot be exactly expressed.[20] So formulated, the matter has an arithmetical ring, but it is of great importance to the wellbeing and progress of geometry; and a century later a writer called proportion "the bond of mathematics." To Eudoxus belongs the credit of the secure establishment of this piece of theory, which is reproduced in Euclid's fifth book, and is still greatly admired by the geometrical connoisseur.

19   Their defective treatment is supposed to be incorporated into Euclic's seventh book of *Elements*.
20   Decimals that neither recur nor terminate, "incommensurables."

Of the two problems to be found in the second book of
the *Elements* the first is—

To divide a given straight line in extreme and mean section.

This particular mode of division excited much interest in
the world of Greek geometry, and received the picturesque
name of the Golden Section, and even sometimes, the Divine
Section. Eudoxus set himself to work out the properties of a
line so divided, and arrived at many results. The originality
of Eudoxus is noticeable in his invention of a figure-of-eight
curve to illustrate the forward and backward motion of the
planets; but it is best seen in his anticipation of Sir Isaac
Newton. After his own manner, he laid the foundations of
the calculus, though no great progress was made for twenty
centuries afterwards.[21] His association with Archytas in the
solution of a famous problem has already been observed.

Eudoxus was a lover of experimental as well as of abstract
truth, and he has been called "the father of true astronomical
science." The nature of the sun was a favourite topic for the
freehand speculations of his contemporaries, but Eudoxus con-
tented himself with declaring "that he would willingly undergo
the fate of Phaethon,[22] if by so doing he could ascertain the
sun's nature, magnitude, and form." Such an expression of
the true scientific spirit of enquiry it would not be easy to
surpass, and, moreover, it was no after-dinner epigram in his
case. There is warrant for seeing in Eudoxus "something quite

---

21   Reference is intended to the principle of Eudoxus which formed the basis of the method
of exhaustions employed by Archimedes. This principle is closely allied to that expounded by Newton
at the beginning of his "Principia" (A.D. 1687).
22   Who was scorched to death in the fires of the sun.

new—the first appearance in the history of the world of the Man of Science."[23]

The gap between Eudoxus and Euclid is filled by Menxechmus (375-325 B.C.). He was a pupil of the former, and succeeded him as head of his college; at some time or other he taught Alexander the Great. There is a story that the latter, in a youthful hurry to conquer the world, requested his tutor to make more rapid progress through his mathematical studies to which Menxechmus retorted, "Sir, in the country there are royal roads and there are private roads, but in geometry all must travel by one—the same road!" It has been seen that Menxechmus came into contact with Plato at the Academy, and this completes the little that is certain about his personal life.

In geometry most of his work was devoted to criticising and polishing older things but his chief claim to immortality rests upon his discovery and use of a new sort of curve, the "conic." These famous curves derive their name from the fact that they can be obtained by cutting a cone, straight through but obliquely. They occur in nature in many ways: the paths of the earth around the sun, of a comet, of a cricket-ball thrown in the air, are all conics: and so is that curve which is seen in a cup of tea stirred round and round. Menxechmus was not thus led to their investigation, but sought in them assistance towards the solution of the Delian Problem, which was then challenging the mathematical world.[24]

A trifling matter this "conic" must have seemed to Alexander the Great, bent on the conquest of the world. Of

23   These are the words of Mr. Allman in his work already cited: see p. 137.
24   See below, Chapter X.

what conceivable use, he might petulantly inquire, could old Menechmus' academic playthings be on the field of battle? And yet the modern science of gunnery is based on the knowledge which Menxechmus acquired in his study. More than this, the advance of science, and therewith the whole scheme of modern invention, could not have come about except for the "useless" knowledge piled up by Menxechmus and his successors.

Two more names deserve to be placed on record. Eudemus, who died about 290 B.C., affirms that Euclid took from Thextetus materials for much of his tenth and thirteenth books, and in the latter he also derived help from Aristrus. It would be unfair to their memories not to record Euclid's indebtedness to these two workers.

CHAPTER VI

EUCLID THE IMMORTAL
(300-250 B.C.)

King of kings,
Look on my works, ye mighty, and despair!
SHELLEY.

IT was in the year 332 B.C. that Alexander the Great founded on the bare sands of the Nile Delta the new city which, as already said, was called after his own name. Few cities surpass Alexandria in point of historic interest. Like its founder, it sprang at one bound into a position of unique eminence. In culture and wealth it speedily defied all rivalry, though Alexander himself did not survive to witness its wonderful success. With tragical suddenness his victorious course was ended by fever in the year following the foundation of the city which was to perpetuate his name. His age was then but thirty-two—the sacred Bull might have licked his robe, indeed!

Egypt now came under the sway of a dynasty of kings, of whom the first, Ptolemy the Guardian, raised Alexandria to a commercial city of the highest rank. In his reign, also, were made the beginnings of a vast and precious Library, the burning of which, nearly a thousand years later, has been reckoned a superlatively heavy blow to the cause of scholarship. Immediately before his death in 301 B.C., Ptolemy founded the University of Alexandria, in which the first professor of mathematics was Euclid. It may have been very largely the ability and influence of Euclid which left Alexandria the mathematical centre of the world for centuries upon centuries. After his professoriate there was comparatively no geometry outside Alexandria and if the fame of the University for Greek culture was great, its mathematical reputation was supreme.

There is a well-known story about Euclid and Ptolemy the First, that the latter though interested in geometry was impatient, as monarchs sometimes are. He pettishly enquired of Euclid whether there was not a shorter way of learning geometry than through the *Elements* whereupon the Elementist stiffly replied that there was no other royal road to geometry. If this story is authentic, [25] it furnishes a little precise information: for, since Ptolemy I. died in 301, Euclid must have been established as an Alexandrian teacher about 300 B.C. Perhaps the *Elements* were projected at this time, though this is quite uncertain still it will be safe to infer that Euclid was at least in the early prime of life three centuries before the Christian era.

This surmise is verified by the remark of an historian, that Euclid was "not much younger" than the disciples of Plato, and "older" than Archimedes and Eratosthenes, who were his "contemporaries." Since the latter were born about 280 B.C., it becomes necessary to assume that Euclid was still living twenty years later. And again, there is no reason, hitherto alleged, for believing him older than forty in the year 300 B.C. Thus

25   No doubt it is. The story about Alexander is similar, but the point is different. A royal road would be especially good going much better, at least, than the average or private road. It is somewhat provoking that this Ptolemy- Euclid story is also told so that its point is the same as that of the Alexander-Mensechmus story.

Euclid's life may have stretched from 340 to 260 B.C., and in that case his span of years would exceed the proverbial limit by ten—not an unlikely thing, for the Arabs had a tradition of Euclid as "a gentle and kindly old man."

De Morgan, always either witty or acute, held an ingenious view about the *Elements* which deserves mention. He declared that it sometimes struck him as likely that "the *Elements* were his (Euclid's) last work, and that he did not live to revise them." In support of this, De Morgan adduced a fact which might possibly escape a casual observation. The tenth book [26] is full of a kind of higher arithmetic; for instance, the one hundred and eighteenth proposition, which any who chance not to be aware of it may be relieved to find to be the last, amounts to this:

> If a square measures a foot each way the number of feet in the diagonal is one plus a fraction which cannot be exactly written down.

Now, De Morgan makes a point of the extraordinary completeness of the book with its one hundred and eighteen propositions, and urges that it must have contained much of Euclid's own work. If Euclid had had the time, he continues, he would have brought the other books up to the same pitch of completeness.

> "This book has a completeness which none of the others, not even the fifth, can boast of; and we could almost suspect that Euclid, having arranged his materials in his own mind, and

---

26   One sometimes hears that this and other "missing" books of Euclid were burnt by the author's wife. The books are not missing, though they are seldom printed nowadays. The story must be an allegory.

having completely elaborated the tenth book, wrote the preceding books after it, and did not live to revise them thoroughly."

These remarks of De Morgan's are suggestive, although it is unnecessary to agree with his conclusions. In the first place, it is surely a very extraordinary piece of fortune that a work of thirteen books, of which only the tenth was "completely elaborated," should acquire and maintain for twenty-two centuries an absolutely unrivalled fame, and blot out every other textbook at all resembling it. And it is not that De Morgan takes a low view of the *Elements*, for he declares elsewhere-

> "The sacred writers excepted, no Greek has been so much read or so variously translated as Euclid."[27]
>
> "The thirteen books of Euclid must have been a tremendous advance, probably even greater than that contained in the *Principia* of Newton."
>
> "No one has ever given so easy and natural a chain of geometrical consequences. There is a never-erring truth in the results."

Well (to continue the argument), if the tenth is the most "completely elaborated" of all the books in the *Elements*, what pinnacle of fame is too lofty for it? And yet it is common knowledge that the book is scarcely ever mentioned, and much less read or commented on: even De Morgan confesses—

> "Of this particular book it must be asserted that it should never be read except by the student versed in algebra, and then not as a part of mathematics, but of the history of mathematics."

27   He then goes on to say: "To this it may be added that there is hardly any book in our language in which the young scholar or the young mathematician can find all the information about this name (Euclid) which its celebrity would make him desire to have." In these words lies the *raison d'être* of this little book.

Then again De Morgan seems to be dazzled and overcome by the immensity of the number 118 to an amusing extent, for "completeness of elaboration' surely is not proportional to number of propositions: this mammoth book is really clumsy and diffuse, and far less compact and crystalline than the rest. The other books may be compared to well-cut gems each with a few large clear facets, whereas the tenth is little changed from the rough stone, and very much needs cutting and polishing.

The view here adopted differs somewhat from De Morgan's: the case may be stated in this way. Doubtless the *Elements* were delivered first as a course of lectures, and were continually being revised and polished. Only at Euclid's death would this process cease, and they would then become stereotyped, except for liberties taken by copyists, editors, and others. Had Euclid worked longer at them, it may be confidently affirmed that he would have diminished rather than increased their bulk.

A pretty story is told of a passage of arms between Euclid and one of his pupils. This young person, who was by way of starting geometry, learned the first theorem, and forth-with pertly inquired how much better off he was for knowing it. Thereupon Euclid called his servant, and bade him, "Give this gentleman half-a-crown, since he can't learn without making money."

More of such stories would be welcome, if only because they display Euclid as a man in a world of men; and it is most regrettable that his personality has lapsed into the limbo of the forgotten. This much has been recorded by a trustworthy writer in Greek, and it confirms the Arabic tradition: "Euclid was most kind and friendly to all those who were able to advance mathematics to any extent, as is right; and by no means disposed to cavil; yet accurate, and no boaster," like a colleague of his.[28]

That so little is known of Euclid's life may be ascribed to a retiring character. What we hear of him suggests a quiet, modest teacher, making no stir, but working steadily in his University, and devoting himself to the life of a student. There have been many such, "furnished with ability, living peaceably in their habitations," and even now the busy world would be unwise to dispense with them. Euclid's long life was fruitful in much geometrical work beside the *Elements*: he wrote on conics, on geometrical fallacies, on curved surfaces, and the like. He also composed a book of riders.[29] Outside the bounds of geometry, he wrote on optics and music.

The number and excellence of his works would be sufficient alone to account for the small impression which Euclid seems to have made on his own generation. Even in a long life his mathematical labours must have occupied such a lion's share of his energies, that he would be debarred thereby from participating in municipal and political affairs. By his day mathematics had become so extensive a science, though most of it was still geometry, that a complete mastery of its range was denied to most men. In earlier days it was otherwise. Eminent men would zestfully embrace the whole of knowledge, and besides devote themselves to civil or military service of the State, in which capacities their personalities sank deep into the popu-

---

28   Apollonius, who certainly had extraordinarily great powers, sufficient to justify a very considerable degree of self-reliance.

29   Euclid is sometimes blamed for not providing exercises in his *Elements*; the fault belongs to the generation which suffered them to fall into disuse.

lar mind. Henceforward, however, there was to be a barrier between public and academic life, broken only at intervals.

In his delightful "History of Mathematics," Mr. Ball relates how Schoolmen of the Middle Ages had their doubts about Euclid, whether there ever were such a person or not. His very name, they shrewdly observed, bore the stamp of the manufactured article. As plain as a pikestaff, it was merely a corruption of Greek words signifying Key-to-Geometry; and this expression, they properly insisted, was well enough for a book, but hardly appropriate as the cognomen of a personage, living or dead.[30] The *Elements* are indeed a key to geometry, and their Greek title conveys this meaning: it would apply to the letters of the alphabet, or might mean "steps,"—and so suggests " A, B, C of Geometry," or "Steps in Geometry." In fact, the *Elements* begin at the beginning, and their first book opens with the simple ideas which came to Thales with the rays of the dawn of geometry.

A complete copy of the *Elements* is something of a rarity at the present day: there are "so many worlds, so much to do," that printers have no time to print, nor readers to read, more than a selected portion. If by chance a complete copy is picked up, it will probably prove to be more than complete, for in it will be fifteen books instead of Euclid's thirteen. The last two are works of supererogation on the part of an editor or two after the Christian epoch: to be precise, the fourteenth and fifteenth books were added by Hypsicles and perhaps

30   The Schoolmen made up in ingenuity what they lacked in humour. Readers of Mr. Baring-Gould's "Curious Myths of the Middle Ages" will recall how he jocularly maintains that Napoleonic history is based on ancient solar myths; and in Mr. Leslie Stephen's "Playground of Europe" there is an entertaining digression on the view which a sceptical posterity may take of the exploits of a certain member of the Alpine Club- to mention no more classical *tours de force*.

Theon, both of Alexandria, the one a century, the other half a millennium after the composition of the genuine thirteen. It may be taken for granted that if thirteen was regarded as an unlucky number by Alexandrian students, fifteen was thought no better. Nowadays, it is very unusual for a scholar to familiarize himself with more than the first six, eleventh, and twelfth books.

Elementary text-books had been written by Hippocrates, Philolaus, and others before Euclid's day, but none of these is extant. The *Elements* resemble some vigorous sapling, springing up amid a circle of trees of lesser vitality, and taking to itself an inordinate share of the nourishment of the soil, the light of the sun, and the winds of heaven: the all but universal rule in lower nature—

> That they should take who have the power,
> And they should keep who can.

Thus Euclid's book stands in isolated majesty: other books, like his but weaker, have come into collision with the *Elements*, all the more violently the more excellent they were, and so have perished utterly. Indisputably Euclid was largely an editor in his *Elements*, but he was also much more than a mere compiler; the discoveries of others, supplemented by his own, were verified, revised, and allocated in his scheme of instruction, and equipped with simple and elegant proofs. Beneath all this, he laid foundations, firm and clear, in the definitions, axioms, and postulates, wherein the beginner is shown the principles he is to assume and the tools he is to employ. On this strong and sure basis he built a four-square edifice of geometrical truth, knit together by a logical sequence, of stones all sound and lasting. And this structure, meet to be the shrine of whatever muse presides over geometry, has weathered the storms of more than a score of centuries. Yet this ancient palace of science has experienced the fate of many a building not so old; it has undergone repairs which are still to finish; and during the past century a pair of wings have been added, to right and to left of the main block.

CHAPTER VII

THE OUTWARDNESS OF THE ELEMENTS
(300 B.C.)

Peak beyond peak, in endless range.
MACAULAY.

GEOMETRY may be helpfully likened to a vast and intricate mountain region, in which each truth is a summit, unattainable without the putting forth of more or less effort. When once reached these summits furnish views which have in them something grand, although it may happen that their attainment conveys the greater reward. But each ascent is only the start of some fresh ascent of a loftier peak, and from no summit yet attained is it possible to gaze all around with every truth of geometry below.

Much of this region has been explored of old, and some part of it has been mapped out. Guidebooks have been written for those who wish to travel extensively amidst its magnificent, if austere, scenery. There are well-recognized routes to all the lower summits, and to the most accessible of these the standard way-book is Euclid's *Elements*. In this work the district considered is divided up into thirteen distinct ranges or groups of hills and mountains, and these thirteen ranges are described in thirteen books, containing directions for making safe and simple ascents of the various peaks, which are within the powers of the athlete. The ascents are graduated to a nicety, so that the tiro in climbing a new summit has to traverse a minimum of fresh and unfamiliar ground.

In the first book forty-eight ascents are detailed: the forty-eight summits, in fact, form the first range according to Euclid's classification. In the second book, however, only fourteen ascents are recorded: the fourteen peaks constitute the second range, loftier than the first, though not all more arduous. Still, no one could attempt to scale them with fair prospect of success who had not accomplished most of the ascents in the first range. Next come the third and fourth ranges, both fairly easy and very attractive. The ascents which occupy the fifth book are not often made by Euclid's routes, though these introduce excellent pieces of climbing. Many who are not expert climbers complain that it is difficult not to lose one's self among the intricate fastnesses of this fifth range. The summits of the sixth range are taxes upon the skill and endurance of old mountaineers who have gone out of training; but to younger climbers they furnish a favourite field for the exercise of agility and judgment.

Nowadays the seventh, eighth, ninth, and tenth ranges are universally overlooked; at all events few avail themselves of Euclid's patient tabulation of feasible routes. Nor are the twelfth and thirteenth ranges often climbed throughout, for old routes have been entirely superseded, and are replaced by funicular railways here, there, and everywhere. The eleventh book is still closely followed and to command success in the expeditions there planned the climber need only have gone over the first six ranges fairly completely.

Travelling among these geometrical summits is full of surprises, and recalls dreamland excursions more than commonplace jaunts on brute earth. As progress is made the view changes with kaleidoscopic rapidity, and peaks that were left behind often leap into sight in unexpected quarters, whilst new peaks spring up to right and to left, whose very existence had been unknown.

An actual excursion may be imagined, say, up the eighth peak of the first range, a well-known mountain, which enjoys a wide reputation, because over it pass routes to countless other summits towering above it. Following Euclid's instructions, the start is made from the plain of Common-sense, with the equipment of the axioms and postulates, and the lowlands of the definitions are skirted. Then a dash is made for the seventh peak, immediately behind and above which rises the eighth. But to surmount the seventh, the fifth peak must be ascended, and this further necessitates taking the third and fourth by the way. To accomplish the third ascent the first two peaks must be conquered. And so it transpires that to reach the eighth summit all the earlier ascents recorded by Euclid must be undertaken, with the exception of the sixth only."[31]

After this study of the guide-book, the route is clear. From the lowlands the traveller proceeds to scale the first, second, and third summits, and then makes for the fifth *via* the fourth;

---

31   If the reader wishes to follow this in more prosaic but definite form, it may be thus expressed. The proof of Euc. i. 8 rests upon i. 7, which again is based upon i. 5. To prove i. 5, i. 3, 4 are necessary and of these i. 3 depends upon i. 2, which follows from i. 1. Thus for the demonstration of i. 8 all the earlier propositions except i. 6 are essential. The reader may find it profitable to trace out the train of logical consequence for other of Euclid's propositions.

having won to its top, he finds to his relief, that the sixth summit can be avoided, and a direct course struck for the seventh, whence a very short and simple climb leads to the highest point of the eighth—his goal.

Here, as in other cases, the route selected by Euclid for perpetuation in his guide-book is by no means the only one possible, and perhaps neither the shortest nor prettiest. There has long been known an alternative route, discovered, as it seems, by a successor of Euclid in the Alexandrian University of some centuries later. The new route does not differ from the old till the fifth summit has been reached, and then an ingenious *d'etour* by the fourth summit leads straight to the goal, without entailing an ascent of the seventh peak. Now, by general consent, this seventh peak, thus skilfully evaded, is devoid of interest except as lying so close to the eighth: it has no path over it except that which leads to the eighth, and the view from its summit is mean and insignificant.[32] Euclid would certainly have incorporated in his guidebook an account of this route, had he been aware of it.

The twenty-ninth summit of the first range forms a pass leading to a most extensive mountain region otherwise inaccessible, but to set foot on it is one of the hardest pieces of climbing in geometry. Viewed from below, the ascent appears fairly simple; and yet all attempts are doomed to failure unless artificial aids are invoked, for the front of the pass is cleft by a yawning crevasse with overhanging edges. To reach the crevasse is a task simple enough for, if the thirteenth summit

32   The alternative proof of Euc. i. 8 will be found in most modern Euclids it is by Philo, or one of his Alexandrian students.

is ascended, and the steps directed towards the twenty-ninth, the traveller arrives on its very brink. The advance from the other side of the crevasse is tantalizingly simple, a mere short stroll to the head of the pass; and atop a view of astonishing extent presents itself, peak beyond peak of unprecedented beauty rising before the eyes. But the crevasse interposes itself, too wide to jump, and only to be crossed by means of a ladder or some such appliance. If the last axiom be brought up, it will be found just long enough to form a bridge, and the passage can then be made, though in great fear and trembling by those who look too closely at the flimsy structure which threatens every moment to precipitate them into a chasm of *non sequitur.*[33]

Abandoning the mountaineering analogy for a moment, pause may be made in order to emphasize the critical significance of the thirty-second proposition of the first book of the *Elements.* The theorem is the corner-stone of geometry; it holds a position unique in interest and importance. Known to the Ancient Thales, it was unproved until the Master Pythagoras, or one of his earlier followers, devised at least the semblance of a demonstration. Certainly it is very plausible that "the angles of a triangle add together to make two right angles;" and yet it has to be confessed, and is best openly acknowledged, that all efforts to demonstrate rigorously this supposed truth are no more than a testimony to its plausibility. First and last, every known proof is invalid because of some plain or hidden

---

33   Only by using Euc. i. 29 can Euc. i. 32 be proved, and all that truth established which, till lately, was thought to form the complete body of geometry. During the past century two passes have been discovered, avoiding the crevasse, and leading into fresh overlands full of new and strange scenery. These passes lie right and left of the above. See below, Chapters XV., XVI.

flaw: in each one there is an inevitable assumption. Euclid, for instance, cannot prove his thirty-second proposition except from his twenty-ninth; his twenty-ninth he cannot prove except by invoking the aid of the parallel-axiom, that—

> If a straight line meet two other straight lines so as to make the two interior angles together less than two right angles, then these two straight lines will intersect.

To most minds this so-called axiom will appear no more axiomatic than the theorem it is used to prove. The question is not whether the parallel-axiom is true or false, but simply whether it is or is not self-evident: whether, in fact, it seems as certain as very existence or sanity: whether it rests on convictions which arise with irresistible force, and cannot be withstood. After these questionings it is a relief to hark back to the indisputable fact that Euclid placed the ponderous assertion among his postulates as something to be conceded, and not among his axioms as something challenging opposition.[34]

With the pride of an enthusiast, Euclid reserves his finest ascent for the close of his first volume. Forty-seventh among the forty-eight peaks of the first range, he places a truth of geometry which cannot fail to excite the keenest admiration. The route to its summit adopted under his guidance is by way of the thirty-second, that wonderful peak at the foot of which a stand may be taken and half the first range and nearly all the higher ranges will be found to be entirely obscured from view by its towering mass.[35] In the first book, indeed, our efforts

---

34   To this topic a return will be made in the following Chapter.

35   Very few propositions after Euc. i. 32 can be proved without its aid, or the assistance of i. 29. Such exceptions are iii. 5 and vi. 33, for instance ; and their paucity may be realized very

are consistently directed towards one goal, corresponding to the proof of the extra- ordinary allegation that the squares drawn on the two shorter sides of a right-angled triangle can be cut up and pieced together so as to form no more and no less than the square drawn on the longest side.

The forty-fifth peak of the first range is eminent in height, and rivals the forty-seventh in furnishing a beautiful and direct route to higher summits. The problem is of a type calculated to delight the Egyptian eye, ever dwelling on plots of land; in fact, the question is one of mensuration, to discover an oblong field which shall be exactly as large as a field of any shape, provided the fences of the latter are straight. This is, *par excellence*, The Problem of the First Book, as the forty-seventh is The Theorem of the First Book. But the thirty-second proposition stands out of all comparison with all other problems or theorems it is of such incomparable significance as to merit the title The Proposition of Euclid's Geometry.

If independent thinkers have rebelled against the thirty-second proposition, it is also true that, in less serious mood, men have cavilled at the twentieth, that—

Two sides of a triangle add together to make a length greater than the third side.

This has appeared to them merely an unnecessarily precise way of formulating what "common-sense" suggests—to wit, that the shortest way from one place to another is along a straight line. Why, then, take the trouble to prove so obvi-

speedily by picking up a Euclid, and examining the backward references. Exercises of this sort are golden keys to the inwardness of the *Elements*.

ous a fact? The answer seems to lie in the principle that the aim of science is to make all truth depend from a number of fundamental principles, and to reduce this number as much as possible.

Passing to the second book the student is confronted by a small but formidable array of theorems about areas. Returning to the mountaineering analogy, the loftiest peak is recognized in the last proposition, which, "as every school-boy knows," is a problem. Its utility is similar to that of the forty-fifth proposition of the first book, but higher in kind. In the earlier problem it was explained how to find an oblong field in area equal to any flat field with straight fences; now it is shown how to find a square field equal in area to the irregular field. The theory of this is the same whether the field have few sides or many; but the step from a field with the greatest conceivable number of straight fences to a field with a curved fence was long in the making. For instance, is it possible to find a square field with an area precisely equal to that of a flat circular field? This is the problem of squaring the circle,[36] which has puzzled the world both ancient and modern, and on which the last word, if it has been said, has been said only very recently.

The peak which comes second in interest is ascended by means of the eleventh proposition; that famous problem of the Golden Section, concerning which Eudoxus wrote a book. Over this summit lies the direct way to the tenth and eleventh peaks of the fourth range, corresponding to the problem of drawing a "regular pentagon" that is, a plane figure with five equal sides and five equal angles and from the highest point of

36   See below, Chapter X.

this peak can be descried, far away but not unapproachable, the loftiest and grandest mountain described by Euclid, of which the ascent is not to be compassed till the thirteen ranges have been traversed. This culmination of Euclid's ambition is once more a problem, that of constructing the dodecahedron, the regular solid with twelve faces all flat, all alike and all equal, each being a regular pentagon.

After this brief survey of the second range the third range invites scrutiny, its summits possess a different charm from those thus far reviewed. The scenery, to speak fancifully, assumes a different aspect, the sharp angular outlines of the one range give place to the smooth rounded contours of the other. The roving attention remarks a change as striking as that between the steep ragged slabs of Snowdon and the gentle flowing screes of Helvellyn. The second book deals with squares and oblongs, but in the third comes the perfect round of the circle—

Not to increase or diminish.

To call the circle a beautiful curve would be an insipid commonplace, for from the dawn of geometry, ever since Thales and Pythagoras, mathematicians have been captivated by its absolute perfection of form. To the mystically inclined the perpendicular was the emblem of unswerving rectitude and purity but the circle, "the foremost, richest, and most perfect of curves," was the symbol of completeness and eternity, of the endless process of generation and renascence in which all things are ever becoming new.

Mention of beauty may serve to start the question,—

Which is the most signally beautiful of geometrical truths? One star excels another in brightness, but the very sun will be, by common consent, a property of the circle selected for particular mention by Dante, that greatest of all exponents of the beautiful. The poet says that Solomon's regal wisdom was not to know—

> If in semicircle there can be
> Triangle other than right-angled made.[37]

There is a divine fitness in the fact that this theorem, that the angle in a semicircle is a right angle, comes down from the very father of geometry.

To the thirty-first peak, then, might well be assigned the palm for perfection of beauty. Turning now to considerations of utility, which of all the thirty-seven theorems of the third range is most traversed on the way to the uplands beyond, and of which will a knowledge best repay the traveller whose time is limited? The twin peaks, twentieth and twenty-first on Euclid's list, and thirty-fifth and thirty-sixth, form a fairly good answer to the question; but the reader is probably disposed to attempt an estimate for himself.

Pressing on rapidly in the perusal of Euclid's voluminous guide-book, and, for shortness' sake, abandoning the analogy hitherto employed, the contents and character of the other books of the *Elements* may be briefly suggested.

The fourth book is occupied in drawing regular figures inside and outside a circle—problems which correspond to

---

37   This reference is owed to Mr. Allman. Dante is an unconscious prophet, for the angle in a semicircle is possibly not exactly a right angle. See below, Chapters XV., XVI.

the fencing of a round field by an assigned number of straight rails of the same length. The tenth and eleventh propositions are triumphs of geometrical research; by a most ingenious use of the Golden Section, Euclid succeeds in drawing accurately that curious and difficult figure, the regular pentagon; to this end the tenth proposition is a direct means. It may be observed that all the propositions of the fourth book are problems: the book is evidently a pendant to the third, and in it is applied the theory developed in the preceding book.

Next comes the fifth book with its theory of proportion; and at first blush the sequence is a little surprising, for the book seems to stand in entire isolation, like the Matterhorn. But the Matterhorn is after all the extremity of a long ridge; and the fifth book is in its proper place, ready to play its part in the great Problem of the Regular Solids which is Euclid's continual end and aim. The mode of treatment, often neglected as it is, has not been surpassed; and it has been seen to be mainly the work of Eudoxus the Illustrious.

When the theory of proportion has been thus carefully and patiently discussed, a great advance is made possible in the sixth book following. There a new world is explored, and all the geometrical theory concerning maps and models and plans is systematically exposed to view. It is usual to speak of things as having "the same shape," and it is with the precise meaning of such expressions that Euclid now concerns himself. Thus, the nineteenth proposition contains a fact most fundamental in the manufacture of machinery from models, or in the measurement of land from maps. To take a definite instance, if a plan be drawn of a flat field surrounded by three straight pieces of fence so that each piece of fence is depicted in the plan with a length a thousandth of its actual length, then the area of the plan will be no more and no less, says Euclid, than a millionth of the area of the field. Such is the nineteenth proposition; and in the twentieth, the same is shown to be true however many fences the field have, only provided that they are all straight.

Now the further question at once suggests itself: If the fence of the field is curved, and not always straight, will the same be true? Suppose, in fact, a flat field in the shape of a circle; a plan of it is made on a scale of a thousandth, so that a circle of a thousandth the radius of the field represents it on paper; then the question is whether the area of the plan is precisely a millionth of the area of the field. It is the easiest thing in the world to answer "Yes," but the best way of proving the affirmative answer vexed the minds of many old geometers: only at the opening of his twelfth book does Euclid give his closely reasoned proof.

To those who are fond of geometry, the twenty-fifth and thirty-first propositions of the sixth book must resemble precious gems. The latter is an extension of that theorem of Pythagoras which has been called The Theorem of the First Book,[38] for Euclid shows that, in the place of squares on the sides of the right-angled triangle, figures with any number of sides and any sort of angles may be taken, provided they are all of the same shape, and two of them may be dissected and pieced together afresh to cover the third.

Besides the thirty-three propositions of the sixth book,

38   Euc. i. 47.

modern editions contain as many as four "resident aliens," distinguished by the letters A, B, C, D. They do not belong to Euclid in any sense, but have been added by an English editor; and it follows as the night the day that English Euclids are to be considered incomplete if they do not: contain these very useful and very timid additions. The last of them, so-called "D," is a powerful theorem taken from the "Great Compilation" of the renowned astronomer, Ptolemy, whose epoch is about four centuries after Euclid.[39]

Not to linger too long over the *Elements*, the leading features of the less-known seven books which remain will be very briefly sketched. At the close of the sixth, an abrupt passage is made from geometry to what is to all intents and purposes arithmetic. Whole numbers furnish the material for discussion, and their treatment runs parallel to that with which younger readers are familiar. The Greatest Common Measure and Least Common Multiple make their appearance, and the theory of numbers is dealt with in forty-one propositions, of which most date back to the Pythagoreans.

The eighth book continues these arithmetical investigations, and the theory of proportion is taken up, but only worked out so far as it applies to whole numbers—a curious abandonment of the higher level of the fifth book.

In book nine, Euclid's theme is once more the theory of numbers, and he engages in the scrutiny of whole numbers which are squares, cubes, and so forth. In particular he studies

---

39   The theorem is probably not of Ptolemy's own discovering; its importance proceeds from the fact that it contains the germ of plane trigonometry, a kind of mensuration which belongs to quite modern times.

"prime" numbers,[40] and shows that there exists an inexhaustible supply of them, "as the sand of the seashore for multitude." With such discussions Euclid fills the thirty-six propositions of this book; and there follow the one hundred and eighteen of the tenth book, in which, despite its diffuseness, there is much admirable matter. Abstruse results are obtained by simplest means, in a manner which has recalled to some minds the hand of Newton in the first book of his *Principia*; and it is a curious fact that Newton's first lemma is nearly identical with Euclid's first proposition of this book. As has been already observed, the book deals with "incommensurables," and ends with a great theorem on the measurement of the diagonal of a square.[41]

Although these four books, from the seventh to the tenth, are rarely if ever studied nowadays, yet the eleventh book continues to hold its own among a crowd of rivals, and has not been ousted from the young scholar's library. Among its definitions will be found descriptions of the five regular solids to which such frequent allusion has been made;[42] and this serves to suggest that Euclid has now ended his treatment of figures in one plane, and that it is no longer plane but solid geometry through which progress is now made. In the eleventh book, then, the relationships of planes, lines, and points are discussed up to the twenty-fourth proposition, and Euclid

40 A "prime" is any whole number into which no other number will divide without remainder; thus 5, 13, 19, 23 are all primes, though 10, 12 and 91 are not.
41 See above, p. 44.
42 Most editions of Euclid give representations of these interesting solids which were thought in bygone days to constitute the beautiful and orderly basis of a world itself at heart beautiful and orderly.

then finds himself able to work out the geometry of "parallelopipeds"—that is to say, of box-shaped solids.

In some ways the twenty-first is the most attractive of the forty propositions of the eleventh book. Suppose any number of straight lines drawn on paper, all meeting in the same point, then a glance shows that the angles each line makes with the next, as the circuit of the point is made, add to make a sum-total of four right angles. But if it be supposed that the lines are not all in the paper—that is, not in the same plane, but arranged instead like the ridges running up to the top of a steeple, or like the ribands in the hands of children winding a Maypole; then the proposition asserts that all the angles each ridge or riband makes with the next, will not add up to so much as four right angles—the sum of the angles will be less than four right angles.

The twelfth book has already come under notice once or twice. Thus the second proposition is that which considers the question of the area of a map, on a particular scale, of a flat field surrounded by a fence in the form of a circle;[43] and in the tenth proposition it is proved that the solid content of a cone is proportional to the product when the area of its base is multiplied by its height, using arithmetical language. These grand theorems rank with that discovery about the sphere which Archimedes chose for his epitaph. The book is quite short; it contains no more than eighteen propositions.

The next is the last of Euclid's books, the thirteenth, the climax of the *Elements*, attained with dogged patience and persevering skill. Everything is now ready; the preliminaries

---

43   The method of exhaustions used in the proof is essentially due to Eudoxus.

are thoroughly arranged; and under the hands of a master, the regular solids evolve in their exquisite forms, the embodiments of symmetry. The tetrahedron, the cube, the octahedron, the icosahedron, and last and greatest triumph the dodecahedron, are in turn constructed and compared; and the comparison of the five forms is the fitting climax of the *Elements*, the last proposition of the last book.

However incomplete an acquaintance is made with the later books, the student and the onlooker will share in a feeling of gladness at so splendid a termination to the *Elements*, relatively both to their writer and to three centuries of painful groping and unselfish toil. Thales, Pythagoras, the Brotherhood, Hippocrates, Eudoxus, Archytas, Menxechmus, and others of a noble band of pioneers, each according to his bent and ability, strove towards a truer knowledge of the forms of things. At the first, a restless curiosity to know the inwardness of the world led them on; to the last, a chastened love of pure knowledge sustained them. There is no need to honour Euclid's name the less because his predecessors are honoured more than in past times. And no one will deride this humble tribute for an empty and vain office of lauding those whose ashes have been scattered for centuries upon centuries; for none can deride so human an act without expressing derision for the common humanity which links man to man across the ages. That is a very partial truth which Gray sings sweetly and paganly—

> Can Honour's voice provoke the silent dust,
> Or Flattery soothe the dull cold ear of Death?

CHAPTER VIII

THE INWARDNESS OF THE ELEMENTS
(300 B.C.)

*If I could understand
What you are, root and all, and all in all.*
TENNYSON.

THE *Elements* afford an excellent illustration of the principle that the simplest things are also the most profound, for those who essay to see beneath the surface, and detect the underlying methods and principles of Euclid's work, are liable to be discouraged because they are so often baffled. It has been said by a mathematician of wide experience that the foundations on which geometry is built present as many and as great difficulties as are to be encountered in the most complex theories of what is called higher mathematics. "The latter," he remarks, "extend in height no further than the former in depth; and height and depth are alike unlimited and unknown."

The difficulty of getting to the bottom of the *Elements* is aggravated by their polish and finish. Set forms and systematic methods are good, no doubt; but the Elementist seems to reach the very acme of formality and systematisation. Everything is cut and dried to a degree that would surprise the reader were it not that custom has so familiarized him with the fact of old. Yet there must be many who can recollect the really repulsive aspect presented by the *Elements* when acquaintance was first made with them. At the outset, the definitions frown from their serried ranks upon the timid tiro; and their opening words have a most dismal and hopeless ring: "A point is that of which there is no part"! There would be excuse for the beginner who should lose patience, and exclaim with King Lear, "Nothing can come of nothing," and incontinently close the offending volume.

Next to the definitions come the postulates, to skip which without pause for deliberation would be a natural impulse; for whether they are necessary or not, they have at least a harmless look. In fact, the reader is not told their essential purpose, nor why there should be precisely three of them, and not thirty-three.

Then follow the axioms, so palpably different in the degrees to which they are axiomatic. The first, for instance, might pass for an obvious necessity of thought: "Things which are equal to the same thing are equal to one another." This is so intertwined with human conceptions of things that to doubt it would be to incur the reproach of insanity; at least, so it seems on a first reading. But between this and the last of the axioms a great gulf opens; here, in the parallel-axiom, succeeds a long rigmarole about a straight line falling upon two other straight lines, so as to make the interior angles, etc. To call such a formula an axiom is to do violence to the English mind and the English tongue.

Now come propositions after propositions to a well-nigh indefinite extent; like a dreary row of walnut-shell cottages, all built after the same design, they stretch away before the beginner, at first sight, by no means presenting any resemblance to range upon range of mountain summits. Each proposition has a prescriptive form, and proceeds in general by the same six stages. First, the general enunciation; secondly, the particular enunciation; thirdly, the condition;[44] fourthly, the construction; fifthly, the proof; sixthly, the conclusion. What more iron-bound formalism could easily be conceived? To resume the analogy of a guide-book, the *Elements* do not even possess the literary charm of a Baedeker.

Whatever reasons may have influenced Euclid in giving this adamantine form to his text-book, whether the *Elements* are lecture-notes, or the skeleton outline of an unfinished task, or deliberately thrown into the most clear-cut logical shape,—however this may be, the need of a spoken or written commentary is quite patent. Proclus has incurred rather harsh quips and scoffs for his attempt to supply the need, but no better commentary is extant. In this "Story of Euclid" no more can be effected than a conversational treatment of the axioms and postulates. Before proceeding to this, however, a word or two must be said about Euclid's method of introducing the learner to geometrical things and ideas.

On opening the *Elements*, the eye catches the first definition—

A point is that of which there is no part.

The negative character of this statement renders it difficult

---

44   If such there be—as in Euc. i. 22, that any two of the lines there given be together longer than the third.

of apprehension. Euclid takes his start from the simplest of geometrical forms, the "point;" from points he ascends to the "line," which is, as it were, a series of points; the next step is from lines to the "surface," as though a surface were a series of lines lying side by side. The final stage would be reached by taking a nest of surfaces, one within the other, so as to arrive at the conception of a "solid." Thus, at the topmost rung of the ladder, something comparatively real and familiar is reached; for the idea of a solid is far easier than that of a point, or line, or surface. Perhaps Euclid explained to his pupils that a point by its motion traced out a line, and a line produced a surface, and a surface swept out a solid—just as many a teacher does today.

Yet this way of Euclid's is not the most natural approach to geometrical ideas, and moreover is rather opposed to the principle, a very sound one, of starting from the better known and proceeding to the less familiar. In a textbook for beginners the least abstract ideas naturally come forward first; the idea of a solid is easier than the idea of a point, and ought therefore, if possible, to precede it. Euclid might have begun by remarking that the solid has an inside and an outside; between the two comes the "surface." Dividing a surface into two different parts, the boundary of separation is a "line;" and two parts of a line are separated by "points." In this way, by three successive stages, the point is reached, and on reviewing the process reflection remarks that a "solid" possesses length, breadth, and thickness, and stretches three ways; a "surface" stretches two ways, and has only length and breadth; whilst a "line" stretches one way only, and has length without breadth or depth. Lastly, a "point" stretches no way at all, and has no extension; it cannot be divided; in Euclid's words, it has "no part."

Thus far, divergence from the *Elements* may be described as a matter of taste; it is of much greater moment to adopt good definitions for the straight line and plane surface. In fact, it is not at all optional how straightness and planeness are defined, and they who abandon Euclid must beware of falling into a worse error. These are his words:—

Def. 4.-A straight line is one which lies evenly with respect to the points on it.

Def. 7.-A plane surface is one which lies evenly with respect to the straight lines in it.

In these their true forms, the resemblance of the two definitions is noteworthy; by substituting "plane surface" for "straight line," and "straight line" for "point," the former definition is transformed into the latter. A thorough discussion cannot be essayed, but one or two features of the matter deserve notice.

In the first place, it must be inquired what "evenly" means, and when a line lies evenly between two of its points, and when it does not for "even" is no easier word than "straight," and the definition is a shelving of the question unless some test of evenness is to hand. Suppose, however, that a line is held by two of its points and twirled round, the two points being kept fixed. As it is thus turned about, the line will generally change its position; but if it should remain in exactly the same place all the while, the line is "even" or "straight;" and so an experimental test of straightness is secured.[45]

In the next place, a presupposition can be detected in Euclid's definition of the plane surface. Clearly it is taken for granted that there are infinitely many straight lines lying in the surface, which again is to lie evenly with respect to them. But how is it to be known that there is a surface of so special a sort that it contains infinitely many straight lines, and also lies evenly with respect to them all? And then, again, what is the precise meaning of "evenly" in this connection? These difficulties are not altogether abolished by the alternative definition usually given:—

A plane surface is one in which any two points being taken the straight line joining them lies wholly in that surface.

It is pertinent to inquire whether there is such a surface, and to request a proof. The matter is of extraordinary difficulty, and it would be a great boon to geometry if such a Gordian knot could be loosed. Although it is not feasible here to go very deeply into the problem, an interesting variation in the mode of introduction of the straight line and plane may be recorded. The new definition of the plane might precede and run:

A plane surface is one which divides space into two halves, identical in all except position.

The definition of the straight line might follow.

A straight line is one which divides a plane into two halves, identical in all except position.

---

45   This method of communicating precision to the idea of straightness is due to the philosopher and mathematician, Leibniz, whose era was about A.D. 1700. It illustrates the fact that geometry is based on experiment.

These suggestions of Leibniz are dedicated to the reader's consideration.

The postulates and axioms require very much and careful attention, and the more so because modern editors of Euclid in their anxiety to quit them like editors, have erred a little. There are few things more certain in the whole range of ancient history than this, that Euclid wrote more than three postulates; and he wrote no more than half a dozen axioms. This is indisputable,[46] and yet the garbling of the *Elements*, which began in uncritical times and under unfortunate circumstances, is perpetuated to an inexcusable extent at the present time.

The facts are these. It is a result of very painstaking and accurate scholarship that Euclid wrote twenty-three definitions, five postulates and five axioms; but modern editions of his *Elements* generously supply thirty-five definitions, three postulates, and as many as twelve axioms. Without excessive censoriousness, it may be termed positively an unpardonable breach of trust to transfer the fourth and fifth postulates of Euclid to a position among the axioms, which they did not originally hold, and have no right to occupy.

Euclid made the following five postulates:

Let it be conceded that-
i. From every point to every point a straight line may be drawn,
ii. And a limited straight line may be produced continuously
   in a straight line,
iii. And for every centre and distance a circle may be described,
iv. And all right angles are equal to one another,

---

46   The textual evidence is much better than for any other secular Greek work; and the evidence of Proclus' commentary drives home the evidence of MSS. See Heiberg's Euclid, Leipzig, 1883.

v. And if a straight line falling upon two straight lines make
the angles within and towards the same parts less than two
right angles, the two straight lines being indefinitely produced meet towards the parts where are the angles less than
two right angles.

The last two postulates are wont to masquerade as "self-
evident truths," and largely because some past editor or other
has "subtly slid into the treason" of preferring his own opinions
to the traditional text.

Apart from what Euclid did actually write—and of this
there can be no serious doubt—it may still be asked: What
claim has the statement, "All right angles are equal" to rank as
an axiom? It is true that the statement is plausible; but an old
geometer wrote very wisely: "We learned from the pioneers
of the science not to lend our minds to plausible conjectures
for the acceptance of geometrical truth." Moreover, plausible
though it be, the statement is scarcely capable of proof; for
suppose two right angles are drawn and to be demonstrated
equal. If one be shifted so that it is in a position to cover the
other, and their equality be tested thereby, a doubt lingers
whether its shape may not have been changed in the shifting.
To take a very familiar instance, but only by way of analogy,
the bubble in a spirit-level is seen to change its shape as it
changes its position under the glass; what grounds exist for
the conviction that a piece of paper, with a right angle drawn
on it, is not distorted, however slightly, in the process of being
shifted from one spot to another? And if this is the state of
the case for a material piece of paper, no more certain conviction can be entertained in respect of the ideal figure termed
a "right angle." It is a riddle; but Euclid stands justified in

placing this brief simple statement among the postulates it is a property of space which he wishes to have conceded him: and the property is this—that space is all of one sameness, no part being different from another.[47]

Supposing space all alike, the conception of equality becomes much simplified; two figures can now be called "equal" if one can be shifted[48] so as to fit the other exactly; but if the first overlaps the second, the first can be called greater than the second. Of course, there is nothing strange in this: it is the familiar practice of the foot-rule turned into theory.

Here, for the sake of the last two, the opportunity of transcribing Euclid's axioms may be seized. Their number is five, and they are styled "universal ideas" by their writer:—

  i. What are equal to the same are also equal to each other,
  ii. And if to equals are added equals, the wholes are equal,
 iii. And if from equals are subtracted equals, the remainders are equal,
  iv. And what coincide with each other, are equal to each other,
  v. And the whole is greater than the part.

The last two axioms are criteria of the equality and inequality of figures. For the sake of definiteness the mind may settle upon two straight rods, and the question be the asked, Which is the longer? According to the convention described above, the answer will be clear if one of the rods is taken and shifted till it lies along the other and has one of its ends at one of the ends of the other rod. If now the other end of the first rod

---

47   In more technical language, Euclid's fourth postulate, that all right angles are equal, implies the homogeneity of space.

48   By any route whatever. Without the fourth postulate the route might require to be specified.

coincides with the other end of the second rod, the two rods are of equal length; but, if the other end of the first rod lies beyond the other end of the second, the first rod is called longer than the second. These fourth and fifth axioms of Euclid thus form the basis of measurement.

To return to the last postulate, now called the parallel-axiom, it will be agreed by all that Euclid must have tried to prove it and have failed. It reads like a theorem,[49] and yet defies proof; and, despite persistent efforts by hook and by crook, it is still unproven; further, it is now well known that by reason of the nature of things, the fifth postulate never can be matter of demonstration. Many a proof has been given, rigorous enough, but based on this, that, or the other assumption; and these assumptions are either equally uncertain with, or more fallacious than, the parallel-axiom. The *a priori* being insufficient, experiment must step in; and so once again it is clear that geometry is an experimental science, as really as mechanics or astronomy.

In an elementary book on astronomy it may be postulated for simplicity that the path of the earth around the sun is a circle, whereas that path is not a true circle: or the path may be postulated, a little more accurately, to be an ellipse, whereas strictly it is not even an ellipse: in both cases the postulate adopted is based on experimental fact, which is more or less exactly known and followed. Now, in an elementary book on geometry like the *Elements*, it is equally right and fair to lay down the fifth postulate for simplicity's sake. In point of

49   Compare Euc. i. 17, which is the converse statement. Very curiously, even Euc. i. 17 cannot be proved universally true, apart from experiment. In the Left Case, to be mentioned later (Chapter XVI.), the parallel-axiom is untrue; in the Right Case, Euc. i. 17 is not always true.

fact experience has displayed its approximate truth in nature, though more refined experiment may, or may not, show it to need slight correction. For most practical and theoretical purposes the earth moves in an ellipse around the sun; and for nearly all purposes, practical and theoretical, the fifth postulate (parallel-axiom) is correct. The error cannot affect human lives very greatly for good or for ill; but some of those who love truth for truth's sake, will love it even to a twentieth place of decimals!

In succinct terms then: The statement, that "if a straight line falling upon two other straight lines make the angles within and towards the same parts less than two right angles, then the two straight lines being indefinitely produced meet towards the parts where are the angles less than two right angles," was written by Euclid among the postulates as something to be conceded, although at the present time it is often misplaced among the axioms and dubbed the "parallel-axiom." It has not been, and cannot be, demonstrated to be necessarily true theoretically; and it has not been, and cannot be, demonstrated to be necessarily true practically. It amounts to the assertion that the angles of a triangle add together to make precisely two right angles; and this latter assertion is equally incapable of proof, whether theoretical or practical.

In conclusion, a crowning fact remains to be noted, that more than a score of centuries have tardily justified the supreme sagacity of Euclid in writing his fourth and fifth postulates. They were alienated from their native soil for a great part of that period, and transplanted among the axioms; now, at last, they are being restored to their proper and pristine place. Euclid's correct treatment of these two postulates is an intellectual triumph that can rarely have been surpassed in the history of thought.

CHAPTER IX

THE GREAT GEOMETER
(250 B.C.-400 A.D.)

Ever reaping something new:
That which they have done but earnest of the things that they
shall do.

TENNYSON.

Having now traced the history of the pioneers of Euclid, and scrutinized to whatever depth the structure of the *Elements*, it remains to depict the fortunes of this extraordinary book down to the present new-born century. So far a fairly comprehensive history of geometry has been attempted, but henceforward it will not be the purpose of this book to pursue all the labyrinthine intricacies of geometry in general; the endeavour will be made to review only so much as has a direct bearing upon the *Elements*.

A skilled teacher may be expected to have the happiness to find among his pupils at least one able someday to take his place, but Euclid enjoyed no well-earned guerdon of this sort. His successor, Conon, achieved greatest eminence in that he educated one of the very greatest mathematicians of all time, a genius of equal rank with Newton or Lagrange,[50] the great Archimedes.

Archimedes was born (287 B.C.) during Euclid's lifetime in Syracuse, the chief town of Sicily. Many tales are told of his marvellous readiness in mechanical invention, and of the astonishing range of his intellectual powers. One of the most romantic stories in the history of war or mathematics tells of his defence of his native city against the strenuous attacks conducted by the great Roman general, Marcellus, whose assault was directed by land and sea. "For three years the genius of one man held Marcellus' army in check." The infinite resourcefulness of the geometer awakened the lively admiration of the Roman leader, who is said to have declared that Archimedes "surpassed all hundred-handed giants mentioned in poets' fables." During the protracted siege Roman galleys are reported to have been burned and shattered by mirrors and catapults, all the devices of a single mind. The death of Archimedes at the hands of some hasty soldier, when Syracuse did at last fall (212 B.C.), caused great sorrow to the generous conqueror.

It is for his services to mechanics that Archimedes is best known. His theory of the lever led him to the daring declaration, "Give me somewhere to stand, and I will move the earth." For sheer audacity this is hardly surpassed by his scheme for counting the sand on the seashore, all those grains which have furnished writers of every age with a never hackneyed expression for the numberless. The well-known story of his

---

50   The years 1687 and 1788, a century apart, may be associated with the names of these English and French princes among mathematicians.

chancing to observe, whilst using the public baths, a principle about liquids for which he had been racking his head, and forthwith rushing off to his study to work out the idea, is worth recalling: even in so trifling an incident a warm and impulsive temperament and a wholehearted devotion to science may evince themselves.

Archimedes' contributions to geometry are here of more direct concern than his mechanical discoveries, but it will not be possible to follow him in his excursions into higher regions of conics and half-regular solids. He was very successful in applying the method of exhaustions, which was all the calculus the world could boast from the days of Eudoxus to those of Newton. His proudest achievement was the finding of the volume of the sphere, a problem which may be compared to the determination of the number of cubic feet of gas required to fill a balloon, or of the number of cubic miles of rock and what not composing the earth. With reference to the earth,[51] in fact, his result may be expressed very simply. Imagine a huge cylinder fitted on to the earth, to touch it all the way round the equator. Suppose, further, that the flat ends of the cylinder touch the earth at the north and south poles. Now, in that case, the volume of the cylinder is considerably greater than that of the sphere; but there is an exact ratio between the two, for Archimedes proved the extraordinarily simple truth that the volume of the sphere is neither more nor less than two-thirds of the volume of the cylinder. His enthusiasm drove him to give directions that a figure of a sphere within

---

51   Of course, the earth is more nearly orange-shaped than spherical; but, for the nonce, it is supposed to possess the form of a true and perfect sphere.

a cylinder should be carved upon his tombstone; and this expressive epitaph was to be seen for centuries.

Among the younger contemporaries of Archimedes was the brilliant Apollonius, born at Perga (260 B.C.), some three centuries before St. Paul's visit to that town. He was educated at Alexandria, and in due course became a lecturer in the University, his bent being towards the higher geometry which begins where the *Elements* end. Lectures of his were published in the form of a treatise on conics, and this great work, though no longer in actual use, is still recognized as a well-head of knowledge. His treatise was flatteringly styled, "The Crown of Greek Geometry," and Apollonius himself went by the name of the Great Geometer.

One of the letters of Apollonius has been preserved, and possesses human interest; it may be gathered from it that, then as now, books were composed in the intervals of pressing work. The letter is addressed to a brother mathematician, of whom little is known besides, and part of it proceeds:—

> If you and your affairs are progressing as you wish, it is well; I, for my part, am well. When I was near you at Pergamos, I knew that you wanted to know what I had written on conics, and I therefore send you the first book in its revised form.
>
> When I have a little leisure I will send you the rest, for I believe you have not forgotten how I was led to write them at the request of our geometrical friend, Naucrates. This was when he came to see me at Alexandria; and then, you know, whilst I was busy over them, I had to copy them for him, and could not revise them because he was off on a journey.

These books on conics were often edited after Apollonius'

death; and when the flame of Western civilization drooped and flickered through the Middle Ages, the Arabs kept up the study of them, and translated them into their own language, with abundant commentaries. Very recently they have been edited again in English.

Apollonius died about 200 B.C., so that Eratosthenes, whose interesting and pathetic life extended from 275 to 194 B.C., was contemporary with him; and the two were, in fact, intimate friends. The latter was one of those rare combinations of all the excellencies of grace and strength which are the pride of any age. Athlete, mathematician and poet, he secured distinction in each of the three departments of human life. For many years he was the enthusiastic librarian of the Alexandrian University, and probably contributed greatly to the development of this unexampled treasure-house of knowledge. The story goes that his eyesight began to fail him, and in a little while he became totally blind. Divorced from his beloved books by this inexorable stroke of fate, life lost its significance, and he ceased to take food.

As regards his geometrical work, it will be presently seen what part he played in the elucidation of the great problems which stimulated the research of his day.[52]

The name of Hypsicles merits record, for he taught at Alexandria in the second century before Christ, and wrote on the regular solids in continuation of the *Elements*, to which his work became an appendix. Contemporary with him were Nicomedes and Diocles, who discovered ingenious solutions of the Delian Problem, a famous nut to crack. Hipparchus

52   See below, Chapter X.

also belonged to the same century, and proved himself an astronomer of the first rank; probably he was the discoverer of the pregnant theorem, Euc. vi. D, which has been inserted in the *Elements* in modern times.[53]

Passing to the first century before the Christian era, a fascinating figure is dimly visible, like a Merlin in some ghostly wood. Geminus was a mathematician of a remarkably subtle and acute type, as well as a philosopher of note. He wrote a "Review of Mathematics," in which he described and criticized the methods of the master geometers before him in fact, he is one of the first critics, and sifts the heap with the greatest care before adding his own contribution. Most unhappily his work is only known through quotations,[54] of which a fresh store arrived lately from an Arabic source; and the little that is known only serves to create the appetite for much more. Possibly the place of his birth was Rhodes, and probably his death occurred at Rome but lamentably little is known of Geminus and his geometrical work.

Coming down to the Christian era, the times move more slowly still, and of the first, second, and third centuries of Grace there is little to report, except in connection with the names of Menelaus, Ptolemy, and Pappus. As far as geometry is concerned, the late afternoon and evening are near, the day's work is almost done, and the writing-up of the diary begins. Commentaries are written, and manifold musings take the place of active thought. The night of the Dark Ages draws closer, when deep slumber will usurp the throne of mild

---

53   See above, p. 64.
54   For Geminus' estimate of Euclid, see the close of Chapter XI.

MELENCOLIA.
ALBRECHT DÜRER, 1514

contemplation. Euclid is coming to be revered with a pious awe bordering on the superstitious. Generations of youthful students hear the same stereotyped lessons authoritatively taught; teachers care to know little more than their pupils care to learn.

The history of the University of Alexandria at the close of the fourth century would be an interesting pursuit, did it fall within scope. Theon lectured upon the *Elements*, and edited them for posterity. His daughter Hypatia was no less distinguished as a mathematician; her terrible fate is vividly narrated by Charles Kingsley in the novel called by her name. The University fell at the same time, but the Library survived until 640 A.D., when it was burned: the burning of books is stated to have occupied half a year.

CHAPTER X

THE THREE PERENNIAL PROBLEMS
(500 B.C.-1900 A.D.)

Low-seated she leans forward massively
With cheek on clenched left hand, the forearm's might
Erect, its elbow on her rounded knee;
Across a clasped book in her lap the right
Upholds a pair of compasses; she gazes
With full set eyes, but wandering in thick mazes
Of sombre thought beholds no outward sight.
Baffled and beaten back she works on still,
Weary and sick of soul she works the more,
Sustained by her indomitable will;
The hands shall fashion and the brain shall pore,
And all her sorrow shall be turned to labour,
Till Death, the friend-foe, piercing with his sabre
That mighty heart of hearts, ends bitter war.
JAMES THOMSON.

THE *Elements* of Euclid are in a way the long solution of one colossal problem, that of constructing the regular solids; but this problem is excluded from the trio to be described in the present chapter. The three problems to be considered were largely pursued for their own sake, and not for their bearing on that greatest of all problems, the meaning of the universe. To square the circle, to discover a cube with twice the volume of another cube, to divide up any angle into three equal angles,—these were the problems which furnished scope for the ambitions, and material for the talents of centuries of geometers before and after Euclid's day, and which have still not been altogether sapped of interest and difficulty.

At first, any solutions of the problems were welcomed, however cumbrous, provided that they were sound; but in later times, taste became fastidious and "style" was demanded. The highest style was derived from Plato, who held a lofty conception of geometry; to him it was an ideal science not to be polluted by any resort to mechanical constructions. Whatever he himself held, it came to be generally believed that he was for rejecting the aid of all lines except the straight line and circle, because these other lines required apparatus for their description. This, as far as can be gathered, was taken too seriously by later geometers, since apparatus is necessary for the drawing of even simple lines like the straight line or circle. For instance, an ellipse may be drawn by the use of two pins, a loop of string, and a pencil. Passing the loop over the pins which are stuck firmly in the paper, and placing the pencil-point in the bight, an ellipse is drawn simply by moving the pencil so as to keep the string taut. Now, to draw a circle the practical geometer reduces the number of pins to one, and proceeds as before; so that it is difficult to see wherein lies the essential difference between these two constructions. Yet, for a long period, the circle might be used *ad libitum* in solving geometrical problems, whilst the ellipse was taboo. And the bias in favour of ruler and compasses has not yet faded entirely away.

This confinement to ruler and compasses is the secret cause of the failure of untold generations of geometers to solve two of the problems to their satisfaction, and accounts for that

baffling of the mind which furnished Dante with one of his
vivid similes—

> As doth the expert geometer appear
> Who seeks to square the circle, and whose skill
> Finds not the law by which his course to steer.

From the days of the Pythagoreans downward these problems have come under the attention of nearly every geometer
of any standing, and with abundant lack of success, because
more was hoped than could possibly be achieved. Time has
shown, and it is at last a matter of mathematical demonstration, that more complex curves than the straight line and
circle must be used, and so other apparatus besides the ruler
and compasses is necessary.

In glancing over the second book of the *Elements*, it was
seen that the last proposition started the inquiry[55] whether it
might not be possible to draw a square equal in area to a circle,
or, in other words, to find the area of a given circle. This problem enjoys great notoriety, because it is apparently so simple
and really so difficult. It has been attacked or reconnoitred by
all sorts and conditions of men,[56] in all modes and manners,
from Pythagoras the Master down to "circle-squaring" James
Smith. The question is how many times the area of the circle
exceeds the square on its radius, and the answer is universally
called *Pi*,[57] and so to find the exact value of Pi is to square
the circle. Long before Pythagoras, some four thousand years

55   See above, p. 58.
56   In De Morgan's " Budget of Paradoxes" there is great store of good reading for those
interested in the quips and cranks of daring amateurs in this field.
57   That is, Π, the Greek letter for P.

ago, an Egyptian writer, Ahmes, put on record 3 13/81 for the value of Pi. Three thousand years ago, the Jews took it to be 3, a result which gains in simplicity what it loses in accuracy.[58] Two thousand years ago, the Greeks realized their ignorance of the exact value of Pi. One thousand years ago, the number of living men not of Arabic blood, who were capable of expressing a sound opinion, might possibly have been numbered on the fingers. And not until twenty years ago was it proved to be hopeless to try to draw a square of the same area as a circle by the mere use of ruler and compasses.

Looked at arithmetically, Pi is a number which does not "come out" when expressed as a decimal; it refuses to terminate and even to recur. Though enthusiasts have computed its value to five, six, and seven hundred places of decimals, all that can be said is that its value is known to that degree of approximation. The first of Greek philosophers to look into the squaring of the circle was a follower of Thales, named Anaxagoras. He was an astronomer of the fifth century before Christ, and his astronomy is reported to have been the death of him. Having incautiously broached the opinion that the sun might exceed in size the lower end of Greece, he was clapped into prison and condemned to death for impiety. The solicitations of friends procured the boon of his life from the horrified authorities, and the daring revolutionary, discouraged in his astronomical speculations and prevented from his astronomical observations, solaced himself during slow hours

---

58   See I Kings vii. 23 or 2 Chron. iv. 2. "He made the molten sea of ten cubits from brim to brim, round in compass and a line of thirty cubits compassed it round about."

of confinement by vigorous attempts to square the circle how far he was successful does not appear.

A century later, Antiphon the Sophist, who had engaged in frequent disputations with Socrates, made an attack on the problem by a novel method which has not been superseded. Taking a square with its corners on a circle, he chose four fresh points on the circle at equal distances from the nearest corners of the square, and then joining all the eight points, each to the next around the circle, he obtained a figure with eight equal straight sides. This new figure would be nearer in area to the circle than was the square and a sixteen-sided figure obtained in the same kind of way would be still nearer in area to the circle than was the eight-sided figure and so on indefinitely. From this Antiphon argued that it is always possible to draw a square equal in area to any of these figures, however many sides it may have; and therefore he ventured to conclude that it is possible to draw a square to have an area equal to that of the circle.

Antiphon's style of treatment has not been bettered, but he overlooks a crucial point in his argument. For the figure to be precisely equal in area to the circle, it must have no end of sides, and so the construction of the equal square would necessitate no end of work with ruler and compasses;[59] what therefore Antiphon shows is, how to draw a square, not equal in area to a given circle, but as nearly equal as it may please. Yet his method marks an epoch in the history of geometry, and entitles him to rank among the little band of great men who have originated really new ideas.

59　　　Just as in finding the value of Pi as a decimal, no end of arithmetic would be requisite in order to get an exact answer.

Squaring the circle now came to be a nut which every geometer tried his best to crack, though, as far as practical men could see, the result in respect of utility was *nil*. Hippocrates attempted the solution of the problem, but, despite his great talents, was no more successful than in his commercial dealings. Apparently Plato left the matter untouched; and his master Socrates, as would be expected of one who was accredited with the very lukewarm opinion that possibly geometry justified its existence by facilitating land-measurement, contributed nothing. Even the illustrious Eudoxus seems to have made no greater advance than Hippocrates.

Thus it came about that Antiphon's researches awaited completion until Archimedes brought his extraordinary genius to face the problem. Adopting his predecessor's method, he placed outside as well as inside his circle, figures with equal straight sides, and so contrived to enclose the area of the circle between the areas of two such figures. Without committing the error of imagining that in this way the circle could have its area absolutely determined, he emphasized the fact that the circle could be squared to any required degree of exactitude. Not content with this bare assertion, he put it into practice by obtaining the result[60] that Pi is less than 3 ⅐ and greater than 3 ¹⁰⁄₇₁. Thus in theory and practice Archimedes' work is unimpeachable and no advance on this was made for nearly a score of centuries.

The rise of the higher mensuration, called trigonometry, in the last three centuries has provided better means of finding the number Pi; and persons with a passion for figures have

60   Readers fond of arithmetic may find it a pleasant task to verify this statement, Pi being about 3.14159.

devoted large slices of their lives to drawing out its value to hundreds of decimal places. Opposite these devoted computers stands a class of people whose enthusiasm tends to fanaticism "paradoxers," whose name is Legion and sign Confusion. But it is only fair to add that the problem of squaring the circle is the hardest of any that have goaded on successive generations of geometrical students.

The second problem, and it is a worthy second in point of difficulty and interest, is usually styled the Delian Problem, because of the following tradition. The inhabitants of the little island of Delos, the miraculous birthplace of Apollo, were the victims of a horrible plague, and in their trouble had recourse to the shrine of their tutelary god. Apollo declared by his oracle that if the pestilence was to be stayed, his altar must be doubled. Now, his altar was in the form of a cube, and the poor people discovered to their cost that to make a cube twice as large each way was not to satisfy the demand of the angry deity. It became evident that he would be satisfied with nothing else than a new cube whose volume should be just twice that of the old one; and this meant, in the modern way of speaking, a cube greater each way in the ratio of the cube root of 2. But how to find this? There was no algebra or arithmetic to come to their aid, and only the ruler and com- passes were to hand. So the Delians discovered when they applied to Plato for advice, and were referred by him to Eudoxus.

The story verges on the preposterous, but two pieces of fairly reliable information may be extracted from it. First, that in Plato's day (360B.C.) the "duplication of the cube" was a problem well known to the Athenian mathematician; secondly, that Plato's geometrical fame was not always greater than that of Eudoxus.

But the problem itself is older than Plato; in fact, Archytas, the teacher of Eudoxus, used a cylinder in order to solve it. The pupil went a step further in confining the construction to paper, in one plane. It was agreed that he solved the Delian Problem "excellently," but by the aid of lines more complex than the straight line and circle; the fact being that these lines, barred by Plato, were actually necessary if the problem was to have a solution. A generation later, Menxechmus, the pupil of Eudoxus, devised two methods, very powerful and very original, depending upon the use of the simple but wonderful curves which planets and comets follow in their journeys round the sun.

Thus in one century, exceptionally replete with intellectual life, the duplication of the cube was thoroughly threshed out. Trivial in the extreme as one might have thought this problem of the Delians to be, it led to the examination of the curves called conics, which have been of the greatest utility to mankind in the arts of peace and war, whether in the throw of a bridge or in the flight of a shell. The whole of mathematics is bound up with a knowledge of these curves, and without them most of exact science could not subsist.

The third problem of the trio is of less general interest and importance. To bisect an angle was never a hard task; and at a very early date this was effected by ruler and compasses. Obviously it was possible, therefore, to divide an angle into four equal parts, and thence into eight equal parts, and so forth.

The question then might arise, whether an angle could be divided into three equal parts by ruler and compasses. Except for special angles, like the right angle, the impossibility of this has been demonstrated in recent years, and it is proved that more complex lines than those supplied by ruler and compasses are needed indeed, it is a matter of history that the problem was the occasion of the discovery or invention of several beautiful lines, and that it furnished scope for the use of conics. In the fifth century (B.C.), for instance, a certain Hippias invented a line to effect this "trisection of the angle," and this is presumed to have been the first line, other than the straight line and circle, utilized for geometrical purposes.

Other solutions were given by other workers, and these must be passed over in a silence they do not deserve, but it may be worthwhile to mention a problem converse to that of the trisection of the angle. The point at issue is, the number of equal parts into which ruler and compasses are capable of dividing any given angle. Curious answers like 5, 17, and 257 have been found; and the examination of the case of 65,537 equal parts has occupied Herr Hermes for ten years.[61] With the mention of this act of devotion to the minutest interests of geometry this chapter may fittingly close.

---

61   It will not escape the reader familiar with algebraic ideas that these numbers are not fortuitous: they belong to the class $2^n + 1$.

CHAPTER XI

THE LAST OF THE GREEKS
(400-500 A.D.)

And I, the last, go forth companionless,
And the days darken round me, and the years
Among new men, strange faces, other minds.
                    TENNYSON.

THE golden and silvern ages of research and discovery are gone, and the iron and leaden ages have come, when ambition strives no higher, and effort achieves no more, than the composition of commentaries and the multiplication of editions. "Hedged in a backward-gazing world," generations of younger men learn from their elders an altogether exaggerated reverence for the past, amounting to an unwholesome idolatry. Authority begins to assert itself, and free thought cannot unfold its wings, or does so only to fall back exhausted the instant it attempts flight. Wondering and blundering, men live their lives in a maze of fancies, and follow its tedious windings, where a rough common-sense would make a straight path and force its way direct through the flimsy barriers of the pretty and sentimental.

If the new era has in it little that is grand and inspiring, yet there is much that is beautiful and pathetic. In the autumnal decay which bedecks the woodland in magnificent array, more gorgeous than the quiet vigorous green of spring, a parallel may be seen to the qualities of the age; the beauty is that of decay, and the pathos is that of old age. Euclid came where spring and summer met, but Proclus was fated to find autumn fast changing into winter; as the ceaseless cycle of change proceeds on its inevitable course, life dwindles and death approaches. A few centuries of editing, a few centuries of commenting, a few centuries of earnest but incapable and barren work, and whether they are compared to death, to winter or to night, the Dark Ages come "when no man can work."

Whatever estimates may be formed of the calibre of Proclus, whether he is allowed to have been a useful historian or voted a wastrel philosopher, no one will repudiate a quite inestimable debt of gratitude due to him. The world owes to him an extraordinarily full commentary on the first book of the *Elements*; and, though it is true that Proclus' epoch is more remote from Euclid's as is the present time from Magna Carta, yet in his numerous pages is to be found great store of quotations from geometrical writings, and information about the writers themselves, which otherwise might have been quite unknown. Thus Proclus has come to bear to Euclid something of the relation in which Boswell stood to the redoubtable Dr. Johnson; and, like Boswell, he must not be slighted because he has committed the offence of not himself possessing the brilliant talents of his master or patron.

A French critic[62] has it that Proclus "n'est nullement original," and there is cause for gratitude in that Proclus saw fit

62   M. Paul Tannery, "La Géométrie Grecque," 1887.

to keep his originality within bounds. He thought good to give with a free hand to his readers clippings from all sorts of books that were not easily accessible even to them; and as a consequence his contemporaries may have found him useful, whilst at the present day he is invaluable.

The writings of this "indefatigable copyist," as Proclus is too pungently termed, are the quartz bed through which run golden veins of quotations from lost writers. Whether Proclus did contribute a little that was new, or nothing at all, this much is certain, that on his commentary is ultimately based the whole story of Euclid so far as it can be told today. The commentary "is, and must ever be, by far the most important mass of material" available for the critical and historical study of the *Elements*.

Disappointingly little is known of the career of this geometrical philosopher and historian, whose industry so amply compensates for his verbosity.[63] Proclus was born at Constantinople in the year 410A.D., and therefore three or four years before the tragic end of Hypatia he lived to be over seventy. Although educated at Alexandria, his mathematical instructors cannot have been distinguished geometers, and it may be surmised that his philosophical training received more attention than his mathematical education. His extensive acquaintance with geometrical writings suggests that much of his time was spent in the wonderful Library which was still intact.

All his life Proclus must have been a zealous student; and he was also a successful instructor, for the honourable title

---

63   Much of Proclus' commentary seems thin to a modern eye; and yet for his day his treatment of the fifth postulate is very masterly.

of "the Teacher" was regularly added to his name. Teaching occupied the main part of his days, whilst he was head of the Athenian mathematical schools; but his leisure hours were devoted to the production of works on philosophy, grammar, and theology, as well as to the composition of hymns: he was keen beyond the limits of any one subject.

Proclus' mystical turn of mind has been derided much and often, but his views of life were strong enough to support him in sight of death. In fact, during his Athenian career, he became unpopular among some part of the citizens, and a fate like Hypatia's seemed to anxious friends to be impending unless he went into retirement. To their representations he replied: "What do my body matter? When I die, I shall carry away my mind."

The nobility of this utterance is unmistakable,[64] but the following examples of his mystical views on geometry are less easily appreciated

The equilateral triangle is the proximate cause of the three elements, fire, air, and water; but the square is annexed to earth.

The perpendicular is the symbol of unswerving rectitude, of purity, of undefiled power, and such like.

All things eternally consist through the circle of generation.

It is easy to reject rather scornfully these feelings after truth; they are only gropings in the dark; but to watch a mind in the twilight

Stretch lame hands of faith, and grope,

<hr>

64   Those who are attracted towards the personality of Proclus will find in the English translation of his Commentary by T. Taylor, a life by Marinus, containing the materials for intimacy with this high exponent of pagan ideals.

> And gather dust and chaff,

is to feel the cords of humanity drawn tighter. Proclus was neither the first nor the last to strive after the attainment of the perfect way through the purest truth his mind could apprehend. Moreover, it is clear that his outlook on the world is so far confident and trustful that he expects to find beauty to be truth and truth beauty; beneath earthly confusion he discerns a Divine order; but, with its fantastic and grotesque elements, Proclus' view of the world is first-cousin to that which the "modern science" of a past generation ranged so complacently before itself.

The introduction to Proclus' commentary on the first book of the *Elements* falls into two divisions, which are occupied in recounting history and studying method. The first division tells the story of the pioneers of Euclid, the second discusses Euclid's style and method; the kernel of the former is transcribed below from Thomas Taylor's translation,[65] corrected a little in places—

THE RISE OF GEOMETRY.[66]

We must affirm, in conformity with the most general tradition, that geometry was first invented by the Egyptians, deriving its origin from the mensuration of their fields; since this, indeed, was necessary to them on account of the inundation of the Nile washing away the boundaries of the land belonging to each. Nor ought it to seem wonderful that the invention of this as well as of other sciences should receive its commencement from convenience and opportunity, since whatever is carried

---

65   Dedicated to "the sacred majesty of Truth."

66   This sketch would seem to have been drawn by Proclus from two main sources, the "History of Eudemus " (contemporary with Euclid) and the "Review of Geminus" (two centuries after Euclid).

in the circle of generation proceeds from the imperfect to the perfect. A transition, therefore, is not undeservedly made from sense to consideration, and from this to the nobler energies of the intellect. Hence as the certain knowledge of numbers received its origin among the Phoenicians, on account of merchandise and commerce, so geometry was found out among the Egyptians from the distribution of land.

When Thales, therefore, first went into Egypt, he transferred this knowledge thence into Greece; and he invented many things himself, and communicated to his successors the principles of many, some of which were indeed more abstract, but others were attempted in a more intuitional manner. After him, Mamercus, the brother of Stesichorus the poet, is celebrated as one who touched upon, and tasted the study of geometry, and who is mentioned by Hippias the Elean as gaining a reputation in geometry.

But after these Pythagoras changed that philosophy, which is conversant about geometry itself, into the form of a liberal study, considering its principles in a more abstract manner, and investigating its theorems immaterially and intellectually. He likewise invented a theory of incommensurables, and discovered the construction of the cosmical figures. After him came Anaxagoras the Clazomenian, who undertook many things pertaining to geometry and Enopides the Chian was somewhat junior to Anaxagoras; him Plato mentions in his "Rivals," as one who obtained mathematical glory.

To these succeeded Hippocrates the Chian, who found out the squaring of the lunes, and Theodorus the Cyrensean, both of them eminent in geometrical knowledge. The first of these, Hippocrates, also wrote geometrical elements.

Plato, who was posterior to these, caused as well geometry itself as the other mathematical disciplines to receive a remarkable advance on account of the great study he bestowed on their investigation. This he himself manifests, and his books, replete with mathematical discourses, evince; to which we may add that he everywhere displays whatever in them is wonderful, and extends them to philosophy.

And in his time also lived Leodamas the Thasian, Archytas the Tarentine, and Thextetus the Athenian—by whom the number of the theorems was increased, and their arrangement more skilfully effected. Neoclides was junior to Leodamas, and his pupil was Leon, who added many things to those thought of by former generations. So that Leon constructed elements more accurate, both on account of their multitude, and on account of the use which they exhibit; and besides this, he discovered a method for determining when a problem, whose solution is sought for, is possible, and when it is impossible.

Eudoxus the Cnidian, who was somewhat junior to Leon, and the companion of Plato's disciples, first of all rendered more abundant the multitude of those theorems which are called universals and to the three proportions added three others and things relative to a section which received their commencement from Plato he diffused into a richer multitude, employing also analytical methods in their treatment.

Again, Amyclas the Heracleotian, one of Plato's disciples, and Menxechmus the disciple of Eudoxus, but conversant with Plato, and his brother Deinostratus, rendered the whole of geometry yet more perfect. Theudius the Magnesian appears to have excelled in mathematical disciplines as in the rest of philosophy, for he composed elements egregiously, and rendered many particular theorems more universal. Besides, Athenaes the Cyzicine flourished at the same period, and became illustrious in other mathematical disciplines, but especially in geometry. These resorted by turns to the Academy, and employed themselves in joint research. Further, Hermotimus the Colophonian rendered more abundant what was formerly published by Eudoxus and Thextetus, and discovered much of the elements, and wrote concerning some geometrical loci. Philippus the Mendean, a disciple of Plato, and by him inflamed in the mathematical disciplines, engaged in research under Plato's direction, and proposed as the object of his inquiry whatever he thought conduced to the advancement of the Platonic philosophy. And thus far historians describe the growth to perfection of this science.

Now Euclid was not much junior to these. He collected elements, and arranged many of those things which were discovered by Theretetus. Besides, he reduced to invincible demonstration such things as were exhibited by others with a weaker arm. He lived in the times of the first Ptolemy, for Archimedes in his first book mentions Euclid, and the story goes that Euclid was asked by Ptolemy whether there were any shorter way to the attainment of geometry than by his "Elements," and that Euclid answered, there was no other royal path which led to geometry.

Euclid, therefore, was junior to the disciples of Plato, but senior to Eratosthenes and Archimedes; for these latter lived at one and the same time, according to the tradition of Eratosthenes. He was one of the Platonic sect, and familiar with its philosophy, and from hence he appointed the construction and constitution of those figures which are called Platonic as the end and aim of his "Elements."

This is the rough-hewn foundation-stone of what is known of the history of geometry among the Greeks. The "cosmical bodies" and "Platonic figures" are the five regular solids. Some of the names of Euclid's predecessors are regrettably unfamiliar: of Neoclides, Leon, and Leodamas, little further is known.

At first sight the whole of Proclus' historical sketch might be supposed to have been derived from one source; but when it is recollected that Eudemus, whom Proclus is following, was contemporary with Euclid, the break when Euclid is introduced becomes significant. "Thus far," writes Proclus, "historians describe the growth to perfection of this science," that is, as far as Euclid, who survived Eudemus by many years. Thus it is improbable in the last degree that Eudemus either could or did give in his History any extended notice of Euclid, or any critical account of his work. It is then clear why Proclus should make a break; he has come to the end of Eudemus' History and he now opens a fresh work, doubtless the "Review of Geminus," in which Euclid's life and work could not fail to be considered.

Proclus is still following Geminus when a few pages later he eulogizes the *Elements* in these emphatic words:—

In every science it is hard to choose the elements and arrange them in suitable order so that everything else may proceed from them and be referred to them. Of those who have attempted it, some have made their collection too long, others too short:

some have made use of too concise proofs, others have extended their theory to an unconscionable length: some have avoided the *reductio ad absurdum*, and some the method of analogy: whilst some again have contrived prolegomena against those who traverse their first principles. In a word, there have been as many methods as writers.

Now in such an elementary work everything at all superfluous must be avoided which might cause the student to stumble; all that directly concerns and helps towards the end in view must be selected, for this is essential to scientific procedure; and at the same time clearness and brevity must be the object of much care, for their opposites are painful to our minds; theorems must be expressed in the most general forms of which they are capable, for half-lights increase the difficulties experienced by the beginner.

In all these respects Euclid's *Elements* will be found to surpass all others. On the one hand, they are useful in giving a complete view of the primary figures (regular solids); and on the other, they are rendered clear and orderly by the steady advance from the simple to the complex, and by the deduction of the theory from accepted axioms (universal ideas). Further, the generality of the demonstration is secured by the procedure through fundamental theorems to what is required to be proved.

Such is the powerful and eloquent testimony of Geminus to the genius of the Elementist, and it is a witness that has been corroborated by the acutest and profoundest geometers of all ages. We cannot wonder that Proclus found the highest contentment in studying and restudying philosophy like Plato's and geometry like Euclid's.

CHAPTER XII

THE DARK AGES
(500-1400 A.D.)

We cannot kindle when we will
The fire which in the heart resides;
The spirit bloweth and is still.
MATTHEW ARNOLD.

BEFORE the death of Proclus, the Dark Ages began for geometry and for all branches of independent thought and research. An utter stagnation of scientific inquiry persisted throughout Europe for the greater part of a thousand years. This indolence or incapacity was not confined to mathematics: everywhere the freshness and vigour of earlier times were conpicuously absent. Rhetoric and dogmatic began to exert a complete and invincible sway. The Middle Ages were a period of restraint for body and mind; if men became serfs as regards their bodies, the condition of their minds was no better. Either slaves or tyrants, in body, mind, and soul, it is hardly strange that there was effected no advance in science deserving approval or even mention.

During those forlorn and wasted years which lie around the Norman Conquest, the flame of scientific zeal was kept from dying outright by the care of a nation which was not Christian and not European. The Arabs had extended the bounds of their empire from Persia along North Africa to include Spain, and among them alone did any remnant survive of the old Greek spirit of inquiry. In alien care the "fair body of geometry" lay not lifeless, but hardly living, like some entranced princess cased in a crystal shrine, gazed at and hardly understood. At Cordova, it seems, the *Elements* were taught in open class in the twelfth century, for an English monk, with an enthusiasm for knowledge bordering upon the heroic, disguised himself as a Mohammedan student, and attended lectures on Euclid there and then.

Elsewhere, in Christian Europe, learning sought refuge in monasteries, where, without the aid of correction or contradiction, it dogmatized in the threefold and fourfold ways.[67] It is of a piece with this that geometry came to consist of a series of statements forced upon the pupil by the authority of an established order extending back to an unassailable antiquity; the student's assent was not elicited by the rigour of a proof, but he was bullied into acquiescence. The *Elements* were cut down to a short set of enunciations; and the proofs were dispensed with, not even being retained as curiosities.

So permeated did men's minds become with this caricature of Euclid's work that at the Renaissance it was generally supposed that the Elementist gave no proofs, and that correct copies of the *Elements* ought to contain none. The eleemosynary bounty in the provision of demonstrations was generally attributed to Theon, a popular error which so excited the indignation of Sir Henry Savile, the founder of the Savilian chair of Geometry at Oxford, that he exclaimed, as late as the year 1621—

---

67 The "trivium" and "quadrivium," referred back by tradition to Pythagoras.

O stupid and most ridiculous people, to suppose that any writer would wish his conclusions to be swallowed without proofs!

The beginning of this desperate state of affairs may be referred back to the world-famed Boethius (470-526 A.D.), the Boece whom, in the fourteenth century, Chaucer revered as his master in philosophy.[68] Born about the time of Proclus' death, he belonged to one of the noblest patrician families in the yet imperial city of Rome, and for the best part of his life enjoyed the favour of the Emperor Theodoric. Nevertheless, his end was violent, and he perished through the machinations of political foes.

A treatise on geometry, going by Boethius' name, gave the enunciations of the first book of the *Elements*, and of a few more theorems. This precious work is said to have been divided into books: how many is uncertain, some manuscripts having five, some four, some three, some two: and none of them is supposed to have emanated from Boethius. Apparently a writer of later date used a name which had become renowned throughout Europe in order that it might impute to his work a popularity which its merits might not have secured for it.

To the sixth century belong two typical workers, Isidorus of Miletus, and Cassiodorus of Rome. The former of these was an architect, and wrote a treatise on "practical" geometry for "practical" students; the latter laid down afresh the permanent way to knowledge, a kind of tramway to intellectual sufficiency, by writing out the threefold way of grammar, logic, and rhetoric, as well as the fourfold way of arithmetic,

68   See his wonderful poem, The Hous of Fame.

geometry, music, and astronomy. These courses, the "trivium" and "quadrivium," came to be regarded as constituting the whole of education, and during the Middle Ages Cassiodorus' works were standard. On such husks the starved and stunted mind was fain to feed.

The darkness now grows thicker, and only for a moment does a star gleam here or there. At the opening of the eighth century a beloved Englishman, the Venerable Bede, devoted some of his leisure from ecclesiastical studies to the further-ance of geometry; he composed a little tract, "On Circles," and wrote on arithmetic and geometry. In the middle of the century, the learned Alcuin was being educated at York, and prepared for the lofty future which awaited him at the court of Charlemagne. Despite his scholarly eminence, it may be doubted whether he knew his Euclid much farther or more thoroughly than many a schoolboy of today, though even the latter is still at some distance from Macaulay's ideal.

The latter half of the tenth century displays a striking figure in the Frenchman, Gerbert, described as a monk from the cradle, seeing that when he was a foundling a monastery adopted him. Before he came of age his inquisitive mind had exhausted the contents of the "trivium "and "quadrivium." The monastery, which was his foster-mother, then sent him to Spain, where he is said to have discovered fresh stores of learning under Arabic masters at Barcelona. On his return, an ecclesiastical career of meteoric brilliancy awaited him: within the brief space of eight years he became first abbot, then archbishop, and finally, in 999, Pope, with the title of Sylvester II. Three or four years later he died.

Gerbert wrote a very imperfect treatise on geometry, which contained no proofs. He was the most eminent geometer of his day, however, and the defects of his work are to be censured upon his age rather than upon himself. It has been said of it, with needless cruelty, that it would not "bring reputation to any modern surveyor."

It must not be forgotten that during this period not only the Arabs but the Indians were displaying a greater activity than the Western nations. Between the days of Boethius and Gerbert there was not a little mathematical study among the dominant race in India, vigorous Aryans from the north, who were in some degree kinsmen of the effete Europeans. Contemporary with Cassiodorus flourished Arya-Bhata, and early in the seventh century Brahmagupta held the field; the former surmised that the volume of a pyramid was a half of the base multiplied into the height, a crotchetty fiction which would have distressed Eudoxus. Brahmagupta, however, was acquainted with Pythagoras' theorem,[69] and independently of Greek sources. But their Indian geometry closely resembled the Egyptian rule-of-thumb system; and it was in arithmetic more than in geometry that the Indians won success.

Indian geometers were surpassed at all points by the Arabs, for the latter had the inestimable advantage of intimacy with standard Greek works on geometry and mathematics generally. In their libraries they had copies of Euclid, of Apollonius, of Archimedes, and of Ptolemy, all of which were soon translated into their own language. Lovers of the Arabian Nights may

---

69   The last proposition but one of the first book of the *Elements*, to which such frequent allusion has been made.

discover an interest in the fact that the *Elements* were first done into Arabic when Haroun-al- Raschid was caliph, towards the close of the eighth century, and only a generation or two after Bede had finished his translation of the Gospel into Old English. In the following century Tâbit ibu Kurra himself carried out the translation of the principal works of the four principal Greek mathematicians abovementioned, though the task was of colossal magnitude for a single man. In the ninth or tenth century lived the commentator Anaritius, or, as his name runs in full, Abû'l 'Abbâs al-Fadl ben Hâtim an-Nairizi. His commentary on the *Elements* was unearthed a year or two ago, and published in Germany. Much fresh information about Greek geometry results from it, and in particular Geminus is quoted at some length under the name "Aganis."

It is unnecessary to enumerate the goodly array of Arabic and Persian geometers down to the beginning of the Renaissance only one of them especially claims attention, Nasreddin of Bagdad, the Persian astronomer of the thirteenth century. His commentary on the *Elements* is quoted in a lecture delivered by John Wallis, at Oxford, one summer evening near the time of the Great Plague. It is interesting to compare the acuteness and originality of Nasreddin and Wallis, as representing the extreme East and West.[70] Among the Persians geometry was esteemed to be an important part of culture, and the philosopher and poet of the eleventh century, Omar Khayyam, was accordingly something of a geometer.

The debt owing to the Arabs arises mainly from their pre-

---

70   The attempt of Nasreddin to prove Euclid's fifth postulate is rendered nugatory by a slip in logic; Wallis' essay is impeccable, so far as it goes.

serving geometrical knowledge from complete neglect during the Middle Ages, and their study did not lack intelligence and profundity but in respect of their fresh contributions to knowledge it has been asserted that—

> If we compare what the Arabs and Persians achieved in five or six hundred years with what the Westerns (that is, Greeks) did in four centuries, we shall find that the ratio comes very near zero. If we owe one to the Arabs, we owe a hundred thousand to the Greeks.[71]

The nature of this indebtedness is suggested by the story of Adelhard, the monk of Bath, whose enthusiasm for science led him into Spain, disguised as a Mohammedan student, where he attended lectures on the *Elements*. His notes were widely circulated on his safe return, and later in the twelfth century an Italian, Gerard of Cremona, translated the *Elements* from the Arabic. This achievement, if less romantic than Adelhard's, must be reckoned an inestimable gain towards the reinstatement of Euclid among Western studies.

In the thirteenth century a Yorkshire gentleman, John de Holywood, or, as his name becomes in Latinized form, Sacrobosco, composed a treatise on the "Sphere" (A.D. 1256), and his little work acquired a European circulation. In the same century a manuscript edition of the *Elements* in Latin was made by Giovanni Campano, a Parisian ecclesiastic. Its relation to Adelhard's notes is a vexed question, but it seems highly probable that Campano made use of them and added a good deal of his own. The matter is not devoid of interest,

---

71 See M. Marie, Histoire des Sciences, 1883, a very compendious book, but severely criticized by Mr. Allman.

because the first printed copies of the *Elements* were professedly based upon the written edition of Campano, and it would be pleasant to find an Englishman directly concerned therein.

Geometry now begins to be emancipated from its applications, although, like the rest of mathematics, it was long subservient to the calendar: almanacks, and sun-dials, their construction and use. Later, with the revival of trading across the seas, geometry was considered to possess interest, so far as it made navigation easier and safer. But with the invention of printing there comes a great awakening: truth for truth's sake, is once more a cry that does not make its appeal in vain.

CHAPTER XIII

THE FIRST PRINTED EUCLIDS
(1400-1600 A.D.)

High-piled books, in charact'ry,
Hold like full garners the full-ripen'd grain.

KEATS.

LET the reader imagine himself paying a visit to some old library, where volumes have accumulated steadily since Guttenberg's epoch-making invention. By a sort of paradox, the oldest books will generally be the largest, for it was in the enthusiasm of a new opportunity that these noble editions were sent forth from generous hands broadcast into the eager world of the fifteenth century. Masterpieces of thought were fittingly embodied in masterpieces of the printer's and binder's art.

Thus the earliest books are mainly massive tomes, unsurpassable for their typography, intended for the use of no particular age, but for all time: on subjects of lasting interest and importance, and sometimes the expression of a life's weary labour. Their appearance is neither pretty nor charming nor attractive; indeed it is distinctly austere, and yet able to communicate a sober joy to the sympathetic mind. They stand in majestic silence, these ancient monarchs in the world of books, like Pharaohs in their royal mummy-cases, though needing only a touch to start into life again.

Romantic musings like these are not altogether dispelled by turning over the prosaic pages of the catalogue, wherein, under Euclid's name, may probably be discovered a goodly list of editions. Approach to the shelves enables the visitor to inspect their elaborate frontispieces, their courteous dedications, their gentle appeals and kindly farewells to "the unfeigned lover of truth," their modest deprecations and apologies: it is another world, not the bustling, jostling nineteenth-twentieth century.

Here is a copy of the very first printed edition of Euclid's *Elements*, a substantial folio volume in beautiful black-letter type, issuing neither from Maintz, where the inventor of the "mystic art" first put-up press in 1455, nor from the beloved Abbey, where Caxton first did printing in 1477, but from queenly Venice, in "the year of salvation, 1482." The publisher is named Ratdolt, and the text followed is Campano's, the language throughout being Latin.

Not far off along the shelves may possibly be found another noble tribute to the worth of the *Elements* in the royal volume, hailing from Basel, in Switzerland, and bearing date 1533. The work has survived the fames of its editor, Grynaeus, and its printer, Hervagius, whose names are quite unfamiliar, though this monument of their devotion and labour remains. The folio pages are closely covered with neat letterpress, the black letter of the Venetian edition having been superseded by clearer Roman type, whilst the text itself runs in tiny Greek characters. This first printed Greek text of the *Elements* has an introduction in Latin, the universal language of scholars, and its publication marks an epoch when the world regained its Euclid, not as a filtrate through the Arabic, but in the words which the Elementist himself used.

The volume is stouter than might be expected, and this raises the doubt whether all its pages are devoted to one purpose: it is so, indeed, but the one binding is discovered to enfold two different editions of the *Elements*, the second four years younger than the first, but both belonging to the same printing-house. If curiosity demands an explanation of the fact that a second edition should follow so closely on the heels of the first, the reason proves to be not far to seek. The title-pages are partly identical, but on the latter a new name appears, that of Bartholomew Zambert, of Venice. Zambert's task was the translation of Euclid's Greek into Latin for the benefit of the educated world.

These, then, are the principal first editions of Euclid, all of continental origin; in fact, only through Adelhard can Englishmen claim a national share in this spread of geometrical knowledge. Adelhard, Campano, Grynaeus, Hervagius, Zambert: all are strange names with a touch of the uncouth in them; and yet these were "honoured in their generation, and were the glory of their times." Now, except for this memorial of their books in dusty corners of a few old libraries, they are "perished as though they had never been, and are become as though they had never been born."

From outlandish names and dead languages it is something of a relief to turn to homely King's English. Worthy to rank with the giant editions which have been replaced, is the first English-printed Euclid. The names now encountered have a familiar ring, "Henry Billingsley, Citizen of London," and "Mr. J. Dee," residing at his "poore House at Mortlake." The former is the translator of the *Elements* into English, and the latter contributes a remarkable introduction; the printer is John Daye, of Aldersgate, London. The title-page is quaint: above is a globe to represent the world, bound about with a broad band, apparently to indicate the manner in which knowledge unifies mankind. Below the globe reads the powerful and daring motto—

Virescit Vulnere Veritas,

that is, "Truth grows in strength from the wounds she receives;" and round about the upper half of the page are portrayals of great scientists of olden time, Ptolemy the astronomer Strabo the geographer, and others. In the lower half, four muses preside over the four branches of education-geometry, astronomy, arithmetic, music-which go to compose the "quadrivium." At the foot is the notification—

Imprinted at London by John Daye.

Within the bordering, the title proceeds as follows:—

THE ELEMENTS OF GEOMETRIE

of the most auncient Philosopher
EUCLIDE of Megara.
Faithfully (now first) translated into the Englishe toung,
by H. Billingsley, Citizen of London.
Whereunto are annexed certaine
Scholies, Annotations and Inuentions,
of the best Mathematicians,
both of time past, and in this our age.

With a very fruitfull Preface made by M. I. Dee
specifying the chiefe Mathematicall Sciences, what
they are, and whereunto commodious : where, also,
are disclosed certain new Secrets Mathematicall
and Mechanicall, untill these our daies, greatly missed.

The last page is numbered 465, and has a medallion portrait of the publisher, John Daye, encircled by his motto—

Liefe is Deathe and Deathe is Liefe.

Then below follows the note-

AT LONDON.

Printed by John Daye, dwelling
ouer Aldersgate beneath S. Martins.
These Bookes are to be solde at
his shop under the gate.
1570.

It is interesting to note how the personality of the publisher, as well as that of the author, associated itself with the book which they jointly produced.

Plain Henry Billingsley[72] writes a plain note, "The Translator to the Reader," at the beginning of his book. A few paragraphs are reproduced below:

There is, gentle Reader, nothing, the Word of God only set apart, which so much beautifieth and adorneth the soul and mind of man as doth the knowledge of good arts and sciences.

In histories are contained infinite examples of heroical virtues to be of us followed, and horrible vices to be of us eschewed. Many other arts also there are which beautify the mind of man; but of all other none do more garnish and beautify it than those

---

72   It has been asserted that Sir Henry Billingsley had not the scholarship for the task of translating the *Elements*, though he himself states that he did translate them-virescit vulnere veritas.

arts which are called mathematical. Unto the knowledge of which no man can attain without the perfect knowledge and instruction of the principles, grounds and elements of geometry.

Wherefore I have with some charge and great travail faithfully translated into our vulgar tongue, and set abroad in print, this book of Euclid. The fruit and gain which I require for these my pains and travail shall be nothing else but only that thou, gentle Reader, will gratefully accept the same...

Which fruit and gain if I attain unto, it shall encourage me hereafter in such like sort to translate and set abroad some other good authors.

Thus, gentle Reader, farewell.

Overleaf begins the preface by John Dee, an "old forworn Mathematician," as he styles himself. His opening salutation marks the man

TO THE UNFAINED LOVERS

of truthe, and constant Studentes of Noble
Sciences, JOHN DEE of London, hartily
wisheth grace from heauen, and most prosperous success in all their honest attempts and
exercises.

The remarks which follow are by no means confined to geometry; the writer has many shrewd and acute observations to make on the various departments of science. Thus, in respect of astrology, he declares that there are "three sorts of people greatly erring from the truth. Whereof the one is Light Believers, the other Light Despisers, and the third Light Practisers."

In this sententious but kindly vein, John Dee reviews the whole range of mathematical science, and assigns to geometry a supreme rank, because it is "the knowledge of that which is everlasting." Commenting on this dictum of Plato's, he uses words of very exceptional eloquence for which the privilege of repetition may be craved:—

> This was Divine Plato his judgment both of the purposed, chief and perfect use of geometry; and of his second depending derivative commodities. And for us Christian men, a thousand thousand more occasions are to have need of the help of megethological contemplations, whereby to train our imaginations and minds, by little and little, to forsake and abandon the gross and corruptible objects of our outward senses, and to apprehend, by sure doctrine demonstrative, things mathematical.

In conclusion, the writer voices a modest request for the indulgence of his readers, and good wishes for their success, in these genial terms:—

> If haste hath caused my poor pen anywhere to stumble, you will (I am sure), in part of recompence for my earnest and sincere goodwill to pleasure you, consider the rockish huge mountains, and the perilous unbeaten ways which, both night and day for the while, it hath toiled and laboured through to bring you this good news and comfortable proof of virtue's fruit. So, I commit you, unto God's merciful direction, for the rest; heartily beseeching Him to prosper your studies and honest intents to His glory and the commodity of our country. Amen.
> Written at my poor house at Mortlake,
> Anno 1570. February 9.

Thus ends the preface to the first and perhaps the finest of English Euclids.

Henry Billingsley was of humble origin, and though he contrived to study for three years at Oxford, he was afterwards apprenticed to a haberdasher. His mathematical learning was acquired mainly from an Augustinian friar, Whytehead by name, who was "put to his shifts" by the dissolution of the monasteries. Being maintained at Billingsley's charges, the friar taught him all his mathematics, and there is no reason to believe that the good patron was a bad student. Billingsley's career was full of great successes; he acquired wealth as well as culture, became Lord Mayor of London, was knighted, and died at a ripe old age in 1606.

Turning once more to the library shelves, there may perhaps appear a copy of the *Elements* edited by an industrious Italian scholar, Commandinus, and bearing the date 1572. The same scholar translated into Latin selections from Archimedes, Apollonius, Ptolemy, and other Greek geometers. Everything which he translated he supplemented by excellent commentaries.

If a French historian may be credited on such a point, the "most learned professor of the sixteenth century" was of French nationality. The name of this eminent man was La Ramée, which in the scholarly Latin of the time was changed to Ramus. As a boy of eight, the future geometer struggled along to Paris without help of any sort, and came very near sheer starvation. A poor uncle of his, resident in Paris, discovered and rescued him, but could do little for him. At twelve the indomitable lad became a valet in the college of Nazarre, and, as the day was occupied by his duties, studied most of the night. At twenty-one he was granted his M.A. on a thesis that all Aristotle wrote was false, a startling position to maintain, since throughout the Middle Ages Aristotle had been the guiding light of the Schoolmen ; all philosophy started from him, and returned to him. In particular, the theology of the Roman Church was inextricably identified with Aristotle's writings, and the latter therefore possessed all the plenary authority which could be conferred by an unique ecclesiastical organization.

Ramus could not away with any authority, save the authority of the reason, "queen and mistress of authority," and he was disgusted with the dogmatism and stagnancy of scholasticism. But the philosophy of the Schoolmen was not yet to be contemned with impunity, and Ramus' career as a Parisian professor was uniformly troublous. Those in authority at the Sorbonne bitterly opposed him; but, despite the notoriety of his revolutionary views, his pupils were numerous. At last his efforts were successful, and he secured the reform of the University but his religious convictions now began to assert themselves, and he openly allied himself with the Reformers in antagonism to the Catholic Church. In some fit of perfervid zeal he had the images in the chapel of his college destroyed, a piece of iconoclasm which necessitated his retirement to Fontainebleau, whence again he was expelled, and driven from pillar to post by infuriated conservatives.

In 1563 he was able to reoccupy his professional chair at Paris, and his polemical talents found a fresh field of employment against the Jesuits. The Society of Jesus had been founded only thirty years earlier, and yet within a generation of its origin was already so powerful and ambitious as to aim at dominating the ancient University of Paris; Ramus fought against them with tooth and nail.

The last years of his life were more and more stormy. In 1567 he allied himself with Coligny and Condé, and his prospects became desperate. Retiring by turns to Germany and

Switzerland, he returned at last to Paris in 1570, at the Peace of St. Germain, and resumed for a short spell his old professorial duties. But his days were being numbered, and two years later, on the fateful Eve of St. Bartholomew, he underwent a violent death, being specially singled out for assassination by an implacable enemy. Thus, after a life of strife, perished Pierre de la Ramée, one of the first and greatest of the Humanists.

Ramus contributed to geometry a great treatise, composed after Euclid's manner, which was for long a standard work. Although it is diffuse and far from profound, it serves to mark an epoch. Geometry is coming to be studied critically and independently, and not merely copied and learned.

The Jesuits, however, were far from behaving like the proverbial dog in the manger. Though they opposed learning of a certain type, "science falsely so called," they were not slack in supplying a true and complete education, according to their own ideals. Whatever errors are urged against the Jesuits, and urged justly, in regard to their beliefs and practices, this remains to their abiding credit, that they established schools which have scarcely been surpassed for the excellence of their intellectual training. Many are the great Euclids that have issued from their presses, and foremost among these ranks the huge work of Christopherus Clavius, published at Maintz on the Rhine in 1612.

Clavius lived between the years 1537 and 1612; for the last twenty years of his life he lectured on mathematics at Rome. He was signally helpful to Pope Gregory XIII. from the sound advice which he offered on the reformation of the ecclesiastical calendar in 1582; and it must have been a feather in the cap of the Jesuit order to have one of themselves called "the Euclid of the sixteenth century."[73]

> Clavius' learning is of prodigious extent, and as his motto is-
> Brevis esse laboro, obscurus fio:
> Brevity spells obscurity,

he is naturally often prolix. His work opens with quotations from the Fathers, Augustine and one of the Gregories, to display the importance of mathematical studies in the preparation of the mind for theology, the queen of sciences. This plea for geometry, that it justifies its existence by forming a field of exercise for the budding theologian, despite a measure of truth which it may possess, would have made Ramus smile rather grimly.

Whether Ramus' and Clavius' works are contained in the library or not, there is one Euclid which will be there to a certainty, and which will repay examination. This is the great Oxford edition of 1704, edited by David Gregory, who had been elected Savilian Professor of Astronomy thirteen years earlier. It is of noble appearance, and a lasting ornament to the University which produced it. It has its defects; it is not critical ; but the attainment of perfection is not to be lightly demanded.

---

73   A beautifully concise and clear edition of the *Elements*, thoroughly better than Clavius' diffuse work, was published in 1683 at Amsterdam, the editor being A. Tacquet, of the Society of Jesus. The frontispiece of the present book is from the English edition of Tacquet's Euclid brought out in the following century by W. Whiston, Fellow of Clare College, Cambridge.

CHAPTER XIV

THE NEW DAWN

(1600-1800 A.D.)

"What! is not this my place of strength," she cried,
"My spacious mansion built for me,
Whereof the strong foundation-stones were laid
Since my first memory?"
TENNYSON.

THE seventeenth and eighteenth centuries witness to an awakening consciousness of the value of truth. The night is past, and the day at hand, though the twilight is to last for two hundred years.

Sir Henry Savile is the morning star in the new dawn. A Yorkshireman by birth, it was his lot to live under four successive sovereigns he was born, in fact, under Edward the Sixth, and lived well into the reign of James the First, dying at seventy-three. His academic career was distinguished he became Fellow and ultimately Warden of Merton College, Oxford, and for a time held the office of mathematical tutor to Queen Elizabeth. His highest claim to remembrance lies in his foundation of two chairs at Oxford, the Savilian professorships of astronony and geometry, in 1619. In the year preceding his death he published thirteen lectures on the *Elements* before his University, and in the course of these made the memorable utterance "In the most fair frame of geometry there are two defects, two blots."

One of these blots was the parallel-axiom,[74] and indeed it had always been an eyesore to thinking minds until the torpor of the Middle Ages dulled the apprehension of a continent. Thus Savile drew attention to what was old and yet new unable himself to resolve the difficulty, he founded the chair of geometry which goes by his name, and so ensured that sooner or later the blots would be removed.

Nor was it long before a Savilian professor applied himself to the task; John Wallis faced the question in the lecture to which reference has already been made. By education Wallis was a Cambridge man he entered at Emmanuel College, and was elected Fellow of Queens'. In 1649, at the age of thirty-three, he was assigned the Savilian professorship of geometry at Oxford, and resided in that city until his death, at the advanced age of eighty-seven. He was a mathematician of very great eminence in the brilliant era of Newton, and took part in the foundation of the Royal Society in 1660. His devotion to mathematical studies continued without distraction to the close of his life. A quaint item of information concerning him occurs in the memoirs of a contemporary: "I have heard Sir I. Newton say that no old men (excepting Dr. Wallis) love mathematics." The writer is William Whiston, Newton's successor at Cambridge; and it will be remembered that neither Newton nor Whiston was able to resist the attractions of theology, to the consequent abandonment of mathematical work by each.

74   See above, p. 77. The other bore reference to the theory of proportion as developed by Euclid.

This short lecture of Dr. Wallis' was delivered in the evening of July II, 1663. Cautious and penetrative, his essay contributes more to geometrical progress than a score of elaborate treatises of earlier and later times. The point of the lecture is simple; Wallis suggests that the parallel-axiom is not evident of itself, and therefore is not a true axiom. In attempting to prove it, he finds himself only successful in making it rest upon a simpler principle, what may be called the Principle of Drawing to Scale. When it is taken for granted that a model or map can be drawn, an assumption is made, essentially of this sort, that if a triangle be drawn having its sides each precisely twice the sides of another triangle in length, then the two triangles have the same angles, and so are "of the same shape."

This Principle of Drawing to Scale, that triangles with pro-portional sides have equal angles, is deliberately assumed by Wallis, and laid down as a foundation in place of the clumsy parallel-axiom. The new foundation proves perfectly satisfactory in Wallis' hands; and whether the principle is strictly axiomatic or not, it is simple and transparent. Were this short lecture the sole result of Wallis' life,[75] it would be sufficient to immortalize him in the annals of geometry.

About the same time, a less cautious thinker was giving to the world in general, and dedicating to the older University in particular, his views on geometry in particular, and things in general. Thomas Hobbes, who was born at Malmesbury in April, 1588, became the exponent of a robust common sense; his system was attractive, but of no lasting benefit to

---

75   The lecture occupies a few pages in one of three stout folio volumes of Wallis' collected works.

science, for there is no royal road of common sense. Like a more modern writer, Hobbes would call a thing or an idea by an easy and commonplace name, as if that sufficed to render the thing or idea itself commonplace and easy.

As an example of Hobbes' style his book, "On Bodies," published in 1655 may be cited, in which he approaches geometrical ideas by dividing lines into two classes, "strait" and "crooked." The former he defines thus-

A strait line is that whose extreme points cannot be drawn further asunder.

By applying common-sense to this perilous definition, Hobbes succeeds in glozing over several difficulties; and it is well for his reputation that it does not depend on his geometrical achievements.

Sometimes, however, Hobbes hits the nail squarely on the head; thus, respecting Euclid's definition of "parallels," he urges: "How shall a man know that there be straight lines which shall never meet, though both ways infinitely produced?" In other words, how can it be made certain that all straight lines do not meet, and that every straight line that can be drawn in a plane does not meet every other straight line in the same plane? The query is unanswerable, and worthy of a better environment than the saucy "Six Lessons to the Professors of the Mathematics in the University of Oxford." A little further on, Hobbes is guilty of a blunder, excusable but for the ineptly complacent remark: "This is manifestly true, and, most egregious Professors, new, at least to you."

During the course of the following century a curious phenomenon manifests itself abroad. In 1733 another Jesuit made substantial contributions to the progress of geometry, Girolamo Saccheri, professor of mathematics at Milan, who wrote in Latin a work entitled "Euclid cleared from every Blot," intended as an answer to Sir Henry Savile's complaint of a century earlier. In that year the German philosopher, Johann Heinrich Lambert, was a boy of five; but thirty-three years later, in 1766, he brought out in German a volume called "The Theory of Parallel Lines." Both these works, Saccheri's and Lambert's, are mainly concerned to justify the parallel-axiom, by showing that it is impossible to dispense with it and in both occurs the new idea, of supposing for the sake of argument that the parallel-axiom is untrue. Many had tried to prove it, and many had despaired of proving it; but these two thinkers first seriously entertained the possibility of its untruth, though on examination they saw no sufficient reason to question its truth.

The extraordinary thing is that Lambert, in complete ignorance of Saccheri's work, should have gone through almost precisely the same processes of thought as Saccheri a generation before. This is the more surprising, if their works are examined more closely: their ways of approaching the matter are peculiar, and yet nearly identical. They argue that if the parallel-axiom, or something amounting to it, is not assumed, it cannot be proved that the sum of the angles of a triangle is two right angles. If, further, a four-sided figure be drawn to have three of its angles right, it is just as impossible to prove that the fourth angle is right. Now, say Saccheri and Lambert in unison, because of the uncertainty whether this fourth angle is right or not, there are three possible cases: the fourth angle may be acute, or it may be right, or it may be obtuse. Then they prove that whichever alternative is given true in one case will be true in all, and so infer that there are three conceivable sorts of geometry, of which the intermediate sort alone is found to be possible if the parallel-axiom is assumed to represent the truth.[76]

Such is the curious resemblance between the investigations of these two geometers; and the conclusions to which they were led may now be broached.

"It is absolutely certain, as certain as that the sum of the angles of a triangle is two right angles." Sometime or other the reader may have used this comparison, and yet by an irony of fate nothing is less certain than that the sum is precisely two right angles. By no manner of fair means is it possible to prove that what is stated by Euclid in the thirty-second proposition of his first book is more than approximately true. To assume the parallel-axiom, and so prove that the sum is two right angles, is no better than to assume what is thereby proved. And the embarrassment of the conservative is increased by the indisputable fact that not only does theory fail, but even experimental proof of the statement cannot be conceived.

How impossible it would be to prove experimentally that the sum of the angles of a triangle is just two right angles, is not hard to realize. The most precise instruments that man could manufacture could not avail to convince the sceptical mind that in a single triangle the sum of the angles is exactly

76   The possibility of the finiteness of the whole length of a straight line not being entertained. See Chapter XVI.

two right angles. Nor, because if there be a difference it is small in small triangles such as can be drawn on the mother planet, does it at all follow that the difference is inconsiderable for triangles whose corners are at stars, here, there, and there, in the Milky Way.

But, on the other hand, instruments may very well come to such a stage of perfection that it shall be possible to establish beyond the limits of doubt the existence of a difference between two right angles and the sum of the angles of some particular triangle. If measurement can once make this clear for a single triangle, either that the sum of the angles exceeds two right angles or that the sum falls short of two right angles, theory steps in, and furnishes satisfactory proof that the same is true in every triangle, large and small. If the sum of the angles of one triangle is found by actual experiment to exceed two right angles, it is certain that measurement will display the same fact in the case of every triangle: and the same truth will hold no less indubitably if experiment show a deficit instead of an excess in but one triangle.

Thus geometry is essentially threefold: it has three alternatives to consider, which may be called the Right, Centre, and Left Cases, according as a single experiment is successful in showing conclusively that the sum of the angles of any standard triangle respectively exceeds, is equal to, or falls short of, two right angles. Euclid deals with the Centre Case, and with that only; in the other two Cases a curious truth obtains: that the amount by which the sum of the angles of a triangle differs from two right angles is proportional to its area. For a small triangle the amount of this difference is small; for a great triangle it is great: if one triangle has twice the area of another, the first has its difference twice as great as the second.

Such is the Fundamental Theorem of Geometry. Lambert had an inkling of it: and nearly a century afterwards Professor Meikle discovered it independently; but, though that was as early as 1844, he had been forestalled by the colossal genius of a Russian and the brilliant imagination of an Hungarian.

CHAPTER XV

A CENTURY OF LIGHT. I
(1800-1850 A.D.)

The truth should now be better understood;
Old things have been unsettled.
                    WORDSWORTH.

IN entering upon a review of the nineteenth century, with its wonderful record of promise and fulfilment in religious, intellectual, and social life, the gaze alights at once upon a man of gigantic intellectual attainments, whose eminence in the mathematical world gave him an influence, which, widely extended as it was, proved fertile in geometry not less than in other directions.

Carl Friedrich Gauss was the son of a German bricklayer. Born at Brunswick in the year 1777, he came under the notice of the Duke of Brunswick, and the latter secured for him the best of educations. The title of his first great work was refreshingly simple, *Arithmetical Disquisitions* and it is reported to have evoked a sneer from the French Academy, by which Gauss was much hurt; for, like Sir Isaac Newton, a certain mixture of shyness and pride made him peculiarly sensitive to personal slights.

Gauss' share in the reformation of geometry is well illustrated by letters of his, assigned to various epochs of his life.

Thus, in writing to a fellow-astronomer, Bessel, he declared how the revision of the bases of geometry had been in his mind for forty years,[77] but that he had not been able to bring the matter to a head, and was disinclined to publish his unfinished work for fear of "the clamour of the Bootians." This shrinking from the loud criticism of stupid people is another witness to the resemblance between the characters of Gauss and Newton.

One of Gauss' points in the criticism of Euclid is given in a letter written early in life to his Hungarian friend, Wolfgang Bolyai. He there says—

> If it could be proved that a rectilinear triangle could be drawn with area greater than any given area (however great), I should be in a position to prove rigorously the whole of geometry.

That is to say, in such case Euclid's system of geometry would follow without any necessity for resorting to the iniquitous parallel-axiom.

He then proceeds—

> Now, most people would regard this as an axiom; I do not. It would be quite possible that, however distant the corners of the triangle were chosen from one another in space, its area should still be always less than a certain area. And I have more similar propositions, but in none of them do I find anything quite satisfactory.

Such was the state of Gauss' mind in 1799: more than thirty years later his ideas had advanced slowly and surely in a direction away from Euclid, and tending to some more

---

77   That is, since he was a boy of eighteen.

comprehensive scheme of geometry. In the year 1831, after criticizing the views of others, he writes—

> Of my own thoughts, which are in part forty years old, and of which I have hitherto written down nothing so that I have been compelled to work out a good deal of it three or four times over I have begun to write something some weeks ago. I desired, in fact, that it should not perish with me.

Yet it did largely perish with him, for of his "thoughts" no more than glimpses can be caught from letters and reviews, and it is by trenchant criticisms and pregnant suggestions that the fame of Gauss has become as lofty in the story of Euclid as in the story of higher mathematics.[78] A further extract from a letter of his bearing date, November 8, 1824, may be added:—

> The assumption that the sum of the three angles of a triangle is less than two right angles leads to a peculiar geometry, quite different from ours (Euclid's), which is entirely consistent with itself, and which I have developed quite satisfactorily so that I am able to solve any problem in it... The theorems of this geometry seem paradoxical to some extent, and to the amateur mind absurd but further reflection shows that it contains nothing at all impossible. Thus, for example, the three angles of a triangle can be made as small as we please by taking the sides sufficiently long;[79] and moreover the area of the triangle, however long the sides be taken, can never exceed a certain limit, nor indeed ever reach it. All my efforts to discover an inconsistency in this non-Euclidean geometry have been in vain.

78   It has been observed that, after all, Gauss arrived at few definite results, and gave no very cogent proofs of these. On the other hand, Legendre, his French contemporary, published a good many things rather prematurely, and was for ever adulating himself upon his brilliant successes. This contrasts with the attitude of his compatriot, Laplace, who had not got far in reading a solitary paper before the Academy, when he thrust the manuscript into his pocket with the apology, "I must think over the matter a little longer."

79   Gauss can only have been acquainted with the Left Case of geometry: what he says does not apply to the Right Case.

There do not appear in the life of Gauss any especially striking symptoms of that great vital impulse, which throbbed throughout Europe at the opening of the century, manifesting itself here in religion, there in politics, elsewhere in literature, and everywhere spurning dead forms and formulae and formalities. Even in Russia was felt the quickening power of the regenerating pulse which was making old things new. "Few periods in the history of Russian civilization were so brilliant and fruitful as this epoch," declares a Russian writer. A sign of the times was the founding of a mathematical chair in the University of Kasan, on the banks of the river Volga, in the year 1804. The first professor was of German nationality, and an intimate friend of the "giant mathematician," Gauss. Among the earliest pupils of the new professor was a certain N.J. Lobachewski: he was destined to be the successor to the chair.

The young student was fired with lofty ideals. His enthusiasm was inflamed, and his outlook widened, by lectures on the history of mathematics. In some way or other[80] he was irresistibly attracted towards the profound problems at the basis of geometry, and so he participated in a movement that can now be seen to have been European in its extent. Everywhere the space men lived in was proving to be a topic which fascinated their minds.

The task which Lobachewski set himself was titanic. Throwing on one side the notorious parallel-axiom, which ages had failed to make clearer or surer, he rejected it for an unwarrant-

80   Which may reasonably be ascribed to the influence of Gauss, acting indirectly through Bartels, who was Lobachewski's teacher.

able assumption, and then audaciously faced the situation. The parallel-axiom had not been proved; need it be true? With a prophetic instinct which is the hall-mark of genius, Lobachewski entirely discarded the incubus, and began to build up afresh the shrine of geometry so that it need not dread collapse if the parallel-axiom were to fail. Theory and practice went hand in hand: he worked out on paper the theorems of a geometry in which the sum of the angles of a triangle was not two right angles,[81] and he also searched the skies with his telescope to discover on that vast scale some sign of a measurable deviation.

Such, in a few words, was the life work of Lobachewski and the extraordinary force of character which was displayed in his devotion to the task stamped itself upon his features. His taurine face, with its massive forehead and square lines, indicates an indefatigable and invincible will. In the teeth of an opposition sometimes bitter, and an indifference often contemptuous, he continued his researches, devoting himself whole-heartedly to the furtherance of truth. He was the apostle of unlearning, and therefore his lot was neither easy nor pleasant. Yet, as he himself says,—

> The earliest notions in all branches of mathematical knowledge are easy to acquire, but are at first always faulty. Sometime we have to turn back to the beginnings, and then indeed is the time to be critical.

It must not be supposed that Lobachewski was a mere

---

81   Lobachewski confined himself to what has been called in the last Chapter the Left Case-that is, the kind of geometry in which the angles of a triangle add together, always, to make less than two right angles.

N. Lobatschewsky

specialist he wrote essays on liberal education, for instance, which rise to great heights of intellectual aspiration. Thus—

> Education begins in the cradle, and is first a matter of imitation. Then begins the growth of reason, and therewith memory, imagination, and love of beauty. Moreover, there comes the love of self, and of one's neighbour, the desire for glory, the sense of honour, the lust of life. All the appetites, all the talents, all the passions, are perfected by education, and compacted into an harmonious whole, so that the man appears a perfect creation, as though born anew. But education must not suppress and destroy a man's passions or desires. All must be preserved, or human nature will be maimed and hampered, and welfare impaired. We often hear complaints about the passions, but the stronger the passions, the more useful they are to society. It is their abuse or misdirection that does harm.[82]

Lobachewski was in no danger of being a mere speculative dreamer, for he was devoted to experimental science. At one time he took great interest in the variations of the temperature of the soil throughout the seasons, and the information he patiently collected is said to have been found useful for agricultural purposes. Not devoid of business-like capacities, he held the rectorship of his University for thirty years, and discharged his rectorial duties "with peculiar energy and characteristic indefatigability." A lover of architecture, he superintended the erection of many University buildings, and, finding the library of the University in confusion, he set it in order, and had catalogues made and books bought. He arranged also for the regular publication of scientific memoirs, and his

---

82   This and following citations are made from Professor Halsted's translation of the lecture on Lobachewski delivered recently by his successor at Kasan, Professor Vassiliev.

conception of the power of the printing-press is expressed in these bold words—

> An idea born at night in the mind of one person is repeated in the morning thousands of times on paper, and so spread over the habitable globe. As a spark glows and sends its beams instantaneously to remote distances, so the light of the mind, which is the image of the light of day, enlarges itself and strives to shine.

Lobachewski was a great lover of nature. At some distance from Kasan up the Volga is a little village, where the care of gardens and orchards occupied much of his leisure. A melancholy story tells how he planted there a grove of nut-trees, but had a strong premonition that he would never eat their fruit; and the trees first bore fruit soon after his death. All sorts of agricultural, horticultural, and pastoral matters excited his lively interest, and his activity in these pursuits was recognized by a silver medal from the Moscow Imperial Agricultural Society.

> His serious relations to his numerous duties made Lobachewski absorbed, non-communicative, and taciturn; he seemed morose and severe... But under his austere and stern exterior was hidden a true 'love for one's neighbour,' a good heart, a sympathy with all honest aspirations, burning love, real paternal feelings towards the youth of the University.

There is a story of a young clerk observed by Lobachewski to be engaged in reading a mathematical volume behind his counter. With exceptional generosity Lobachewski exerted himself to procure his admission to a grammar school, whence he proceeded to the University, and came to occupy the chair of physics.

Another story tells that the son of a poor Priest travelled afoot from Siberia, and arrived in a destitute state at Kasan. Lobachewski took him under his charge and secured for him a medical education. The favour was not misplaced, for the recipient rose to an honourable position, and evinced his gratitude by the bequest of a valuable library to the University whose rector had so helped him in time of need.

Lobachewski's significance in the story of Euclid is vital. His whole life [83] was devoted to the investigation of the bases of geometry; and the best known of his writings on this topic, "Geometrical Studies in the Theory of Parallels," published in 1840, has been translated into most of the great languages of the globe, English, German, Italian, French, among others. In this little work he elaborates the kind of geometry in which the sum of the angles of a triangle is more or less short of two right angles. To call him the Copernicus of Geometry is not idle flattery, for what Copernicus did for conceptions of the universe, Lobachewski did in a large degree for conceptions of space.

Lobachewski was not alone in the work, and if his genius is admirable, that of John Bolyai is astounding. What the former did by the continued effort of an ample lifetime, the latter seemed to achieve in one flight of the mind. Lobachewski's tenacity may suggest the steady glow of a planet: Bolyai's career is that of a brilliant but transient meteor.

Wolfgang Bolyai, great father of a greater son, was him-

83   He was born in 1793, and died in 1856.

self a geometer of large powers. Of Hungarian birth, he was educated in various German seminaries. In 1797 he resided at Gottingen, where he met Gauss, and a lifelong friendship ensued between the two men. From his secluded position as professor in a Hungarian University,[84] Bolyai continued to correspond with Gauss, and so maintained connection with the hub of the mathematical world. He lectured for nearly half a century, and during that time wrote in Latin an introduction to mathematics, entitled, "An Attempt to introduce Youth to the Fundamentals of Pure Science, Elementary and Advanced, by a clear and proper Method."

This work, published in two large volumes in the year 1832, was the fitting crown of his lifework.

To the first volume was attached an "Appendix showing the absolutely true Science of Space," by the son of the author. Its aim was to work out a system of geometry independent of the question whether the parallel-axiom was true or false: and in it John Bolyai develops, with astonishing power, a geometry precisely like Lobachewski's, though obtained in complete ignorance of the other's work.[85]

The Bolyais, father and son, possessed singular personalities. The elder, Wolfgang, spent some of his leisure in the composition of tragedies; in middle age he translated Pope's "Essay on Man" into Hungarian. Beside this devotion to poetry, he loved music, and played much on the violin. A peculiar hobby of his was the invention and fabrication of

---

84   At Maros-Vasarhely, in Transylvania.
85   The influence of Gauss on the elder, and so indirectly on the younger of the Bolyais, may be noted. The cases of Saccheri and Lambert, and of Lobachewski and Bolyai, are curiously parallel.

ovens of new-fangled patterns, and the domestic economy of Transylvania is said to have been revolutionized by an oven of his contrivance, distinguished by a special arrangement of its flues. The walls of his rooms were adorned with discarded models, interspersed with pet violins. Here and there hung portraits: one of his friend Gauss: another, of Shakespeare, whom he called the "child of nature and a third, of Schiller, who was the "grandchild of Shakespeare."

One who saw him at home, wrote —

Before a plain dinner sat an old squire, in coarse, dark Hungarian breeches, with high boots, a white flannel jacket, a broad-rimmed hat on his head: that was Wolfgang Bolyai. His was a character of great nobility: possessing an immovable faith in the immortality of the soul, he was fond of comparing the earth to a muddy pool, wherein the fettered soul waded until death came, and a releasing angel set the captive free to visit happier realms.

It is reported that he wished his funeral to be simple, and his grave to have no monument, except an apple tree, the fruit of which tree, he thought, had thrice intervened vitally in the history of mankind. The apples of Eve and Paris made a hell of earth but Newton's, by a quaint fancy, he regarded as restoring earth to its original dignity. This grand old man died in the late autumn of 1856.

Not quite so much is recorded of his son, John Bolyai. He was born at the opening of the century, in the year 1802, and on coming of age entered the army as a cadet. At twenty he had become sub-lieutenant, whence in ten years or so he was promoted to a captaincy, though conditionally upon his retirement with the pension assigned to that rank. The circumstances were somewhat as follows. In the garrison where Bolyai was stationed were thirteen brother-officers, who in consequence of some friction simultaneously challenged the sub-lieutenant. It is "matter of history" that the redoubtable Bolyai accepted the batch, with the proviso that between successive duels he should be allowed to play awhile on his violin. The concession made, he vanquished in turn his thirteen opponents. In such a matter the Government was bound to consult its interests, for the placing *hors de combat* of thirteen of its officers, in however gentlemanly a fashion, could not be suffered to recur. Hence it was that promotion and retirement were offered to the gallant lieutenant.

Along with such mastery of the fencing-foil and violin-bow, the younger Bolyai displayed many signs of an unique personality. Towards the end of his life[86] he concerned himself with the colossal idea of an universal language, urging that what was an accomplished fact in music, was not beyond hope in other departments of life.

The disposition of this remarkable man is described as retiring: he lived almost the life of a hermit. Those who encountered him were struck by a strangeness in his ways of acting and thinking,—superficial eccentricities for which his geometrical work amply atones, for in the long run the genuineness of the gold tells, and its grotesque stamp is forgotten.

---

86   He died in 1860, at the age of fifty-eight.

CHAPTER XVI

A CENTURY OF LIGHT. II

(1850-1900 A.D.)

*Nor deem the irrevocable past
As wholly wasted, wholly vain ;
If, rising on its wrecks. at last
To something higher we attain.*
LONGFELLOW.

LIKE many another epigram, Carlyle's terse definition of genius, as "an infinite capacity fo taking pains," suggests much that is false by suppressing something that is true. If genius is almost invariably accompanied by astonishing laboriousness in the cause of truth, the fact remains that the most painstaking of encyclopredical hacks may be positively destitute of genius. A man is no more a genius because he possesses an infinite capacity for taking pains, than a boy who writes up his copybook with infinite pains is bound to rise to the level of even a minor poet. "Genius" resembles "life it is a kind of ebullition of vitality, easy to recognize and hard to define. The word suggests brilliant flashes of intellect, startling bounds of intuition, wherein the mind "between stirrup and ground" conceives and immediately brings to birth a new idea, an entirely fresh notion, which centuries of earth-bound logic and slow-plodding effort might never have begotten.

In the story of Euclid this superhuman gift of "genius" is

well seen in Bernhard Riemann, professor of mathematics in the great German University of Göttingen, and especially in a short inaugural essay read on his assumption of the professorial chair in 1854. The title of the dissertation is, "On the Hypotheses which lie at the Bases of Geometry;" and for brevity[87] it contrasts with the huge folios of a Clavius. Seeming to disdain adornments of style and illustration, Riemann's essay towers like a lofty spire of rugged rock amid lower heights flanked by gentler grassy slopes; of its contents it may be said that their suggestiveness has not yet been exhausted: they have yielded a harvest already in a revolution of geometrical thought, and in the future an aftermath may yet be gathered in.

The epoch-making idea with which Riemann's name will be ever associated in the annals of geometry is contained in a new way of conceiving space as a whole. The whole of space is necessarily conceived as endless, without bound or limit: the existence of a boundary would lead the mind to think of fresh space on the other side of that boundary, which would be contradictory. For space as a whole to have any end or boundary is thus unthinkable but, until Riemann reminded the world of the mistake, it had been universally assumed that because space had no end, it must be infinite. Now, by "infinite" is generally implied more than "endless:" the word "infinite" carries with it the sense of immeasurable greatness, whereas the word "endless" need have no such meaning. For instance, a circle is an endless curve in which a man might walk for ever, and encounter no end; but on that account the circle would not be called infinite.

87   The essay would occupy about 17 pages of this little book. A translation into English was made by Professor Clifford, and will be found among his collected papers.

Since, therefore, "endless" and "infinite" possess different meanings, and the latter implies more than the former, it appears that space, though certainly endless, is not certainly infinite. This is Riemann's point that space is certainly endless, but not certainly infinite. Although it is customary to think of space as extending to infinite distances in every direction, yet it must not be forgotten that what is certain is no more than this, that space comes to no end. And so there arises the conceivable hypothesis, that space may return into itself in some way, and be indeed endless, but not of infinite size.

This distinction between "endless" and "infinite" is not mere pedantry, but when applied to the space of experience is found to lie at the root of one of the greatest discoveries of geometry. In going over the argument once again, it may be found helpful to think of a circular cycle-track. The track is endless, because the cyclist may ride along it indefinitely and never encounter a barrier but the track is not infinite, for however long he continue to ride, the cyclist can attain no further from the start than half a lap measured along the track ever and anon he returns to the starting-point. Now if the track be not circular but perfectly straight it stretches away endlessly, in like manner: yet it may prove not to be infinite in length. It is quite conceivable, in fact, that the cyclist should find himself returning to the starting-point again. In such a case the straight line would not be of infinite length it would be an endless line no less closed than the curved circle though endless, the straight line in its completeness would have a definite length, and this length might be called a "lap."

Riemann's conception will seem preposterous to many

minds until the prejudice which causes it to have so novel and paradoxical an appearance has been eradicated. A circle returns into itself; and that seems only natural, because a circle is curved: but how can a line always absolutely straight return into itself, without somewhere or other undergoing bending?

Perhaps the difficulty resides in the fact that no eye has been able to inspect in its totality a closed line that was not curved, and the mind is permeated by the conviction that what is true for small figures is equally true on a larger scale. The word "scale" proves to be the nucleus of the difficulty, when it is remembered that drawing to scale is not exact when Euclid's geometry is not exact; and that, conversely, if Euclid's system is rejected it is impossible to retain the principle of drawing to scale.[88] Moreover, the larger an object the more imperfect will a small map or model necessarily be. For an extremely large object like a whole straight line, the utter hopelessness of the task of drawing anything like a fair representation to the eye on this or any other page has to be conceded. If the hypothesis of the infinite size of space is abandoned, Euclid's system of geometry is abandoned therewith: the possibility of drawing accurately to scale is repudiated: and a line can be drawn both straight and closed only by drawing it "life-size."

There is another demurrer, albeit of a more technical sort, which may be brought into court against the Riemannian conception of space: the conception presents the appearance, at least, of violating the familiar "axiom," that two straight lines cannot intersect in more than one point. If, for instance, the upright side-strokes of a capital H be taken to represent two

88   See earlier, p. 127.

straight lines having a common perpendicular, indicated by the level cross-stroke, the lines betokened by the side-strokes must of necessity intersect- this being a demonstrable consequence of the hypothesis that their length is not infinite. And yet on whichever side of the cross-stroke, above or below, their intersection lie, there must lie on the opposite side, below or above, another intersection: in fact, however the side-strokes are related to each other on one side of the cross-stroke, in the same way precisely must they be mutually related on the other side. Thus there would seem to be deduced that the two vertical straight lines intersect in two points, the one above, the other below, the horizontal straight line which is perpendicular to both, contrary to the axiom usually laid down.[89]

The difficulty may be evaded, however, in a very simple manner, suggestive of the severance of a Gordian knot: the two points, above and below, may be held to be one and the same point. It is clear, to adopt once more an almost outworn illustration, that two cyclists, who ride with equal speeds in opposite directions, upward and downward, between the side-lines of the figure of H, will meet some time or other; this place of meeting is at the point of intersection of the two side-lines, the "one and the same point" just mentioned.

The antithesis between the system of geometry arising out of Riemann's suggestions and that which is associated with the names of Lobachewski and Bolyai remains to be noted. In the latter, as in the Euclidean system, space is of infinite

89   The postulate: Two straight lines cannot enclose a space, was almost certainly not enunciated by Euclid, although it is generally included among the axioms given in modern editions of the *Elements*.
Use was made of the paradox in the text by Ptolemy, the Greek astronomer, already mentioned on p. 64.

extent; but in the former, the Riemannian, all space is finite in respect of content, and from this it follows mathematically that the sum of the angles of every triangle ever, by more or by less, exceeds two right angles. So the Riemannian theory of space fills the gap left vacant when the other two systems of geometry have been elaborated. In the geometry of Euclid the sum of the angles of each and every triangle is precisely and absolutely two right angles: in the geometry of Lobachewski and Bolyai the sum always falls short of two right angles: and in the geometry initiated by Riemann's views the sum invariably exceeds two right angles.

Thus it transpires that Euclidean geometry is, so to say, the Central Case of three alternatives from it the Lobachewskian and Riemannian differ in opposite directions, and may therefore with some fitness be termed the Left and Right Cases respectively.

At an early stage, then, the royal road of Geometry becomes threefold, and very shortly after his outset the student has to decide which of three paths he will choose to follow. As yet there stands no sign-post to indicate the correct route: the indication can come only from experiment, and the decisive experiment has yet to be made.[90] If in one triangle the sum of the angles is known to be certainly less than, equal to, or greater than two right angles, the same holds good, so theory teaches, for every triangle, and the Left, Central, and Right Cases respectively describe the space of experience, to the

90   Lobachewski stated that he had tried by observations of stars to demonstrate the existence of triangles whose angle-sums fell short of two right angles; he considered that he had been unsuccessful. This refers to the Left Case: as regards the Right, a stellar test is suggested below, p. 154.

exclusion of the remaining pair of hypotheses. Furthermore, in the Left, Central, and Right Cases, there are two, one, and no parallels, respectively, through any point to any straight line; and in the extreme Cases it is noteworthy that the area of a triangle is proportional to the amount of the difference between two right angles and the sum of its angles.[91]

Such has been the development of Geometry up to the opening of this new century. For thousands of years, from Ahmes to Wallis, it hardly entered into the minds of geometers that the Central Case was other than true in fact as well as consistent in theory. All Greek geometry dealt with the Central Case only, and if it was often realized that this Case was demonstrated in a very unsatisfactory manner, its truth was nevertheless considered indubitable. As late as the eighteenth century Saccheri and Lambert awoke to a sense of uneasiness whether there might not be a Left Case and a Right Case, but deliberately decided against the possibility. In the first half of the nineteenth century Lobachewski and Bolyai worked out the Left Case; and in the second half the hint, which Riemann gave out, of the reasonableness of the supposition that space was not of infinite dimensions, was followed up with great vigour and success; proof did not fail to be forthcoming that the three Cases were theoretically on the same footing, and that nothing short of experiment would decide among the trio.

In conclusion, a few features of the Right Case, more or

91   This leads to the conclusion that in the Left and Right Cases the area of a triangle is never of infinite magnitude, a result which surprised Gauss in his study of the Left Case wherein the sides may be of infinite length: see the extract from his letter on p. 136.
In the Right Case the theorem in the text is an obvious inference from the fact that the longest side cannot exceed the whole straight line in length, and so cannot be infinite.

less paradoxical in character, may receive mention: they are consequences of the ancillary facts that in this Case the whole length of a straight line is not of infinite magnitude, and that all straight lines return into themselves.

In the first place, the whole of space is of limited volume, and therefore the number of worlds capable of being packed into it is limited, and so it may be said that the host of stars can be conceived to be enumerated even though the task rival in immensity the labour of computing the grains of sand on the shores of a continent.[92]

In the next place, since the complete straight line has a limited length, which for shortness' sake may be called a "lap," it is clear that every object has two distances, measured forward and backward, which together make up a lap. A star will be visible in two opposite directions in the sky, and a short and simple geometrical argument establishes the fact that these antipodal images are equally bright.[93]

Lastly, in the case of a particular star, the sun, it might fairly be supposed that all doubts could be allayed. Speaking geometrically, if the Right Case is followed, an object like the sun ought to have two images in the heavens, precisely

92   It may be observed that some modern astronomers have expressed disappointment that powerful telescopes do not reveal a much greater store of new stars for registration. Among other explanations, however, the quenching of their light through the mistiness of inter- stellar space would amply suffice to account for the fact.

93   This implies that if the Right Case holds good 'in nature," the celestial sphere is symmetrical about its centre, geometrically speaking. In the realm of astronomical fact, however, the exactitude of antipodality and the equality in brightness of the two images of the star would be impaired, the former from the observer's motion in space, the latter from the effect of interstellar fog.

Conversely, this necessary consequence of the Right Case might serve to attest its applicability to the space of experience: the aberration in position would follow from the star's known distance and some assumed length for the "lap." The diminution in brightness would defy prediction. The identification of the two images by the aid of the spectroscope is probably an impracticable idea.

opposite to each other, and not only of equal size but also of equal brightness. Of course this by no means accords with the observed fact of the alternation of day and night: a new sun does not rise as the old one sets: but the physical circumstances of the actual problem serve to annul the condemnation of the Right Case, which would otherwise have seemed inevitable.[94]

Thus, then, at the close of this brief attempt to narrate the Story of Euclid, Geometry, though first concerned merely with the measurement of land, is seen to be occupied with more ambitious problems in the expanse of the heavens. The Muse stands, with feet placed firm upon the earth, as of yore, but her hands grope among stars and nebulae in the search for a certitude she has yet to find.

In the consideration of these qualifying circumstances I have been much aided by the Rev. P. V. Wodehouse, sometime Fellow of Caius College, Cambridge.

94   The accredited fact of the motion of the solar system through space, along with the certainly great length of the lap, produces a radical displacement in the putative position of the secondary image of the sun, and causes, besides, its diminution to microscopic apparent dimensions. Moreover the mistiness of space would doubtless cause the brightness of the secondary image to be evanescent, and it would therefore seem quixotic to attempt any explanation, on these lines, of either the Gegenschein or zodiacal light.